ORC'S TAMING

MONSTER MATE HUNT, BOOK 5

AVA ROSS

ENCHANTED STAR PRESS

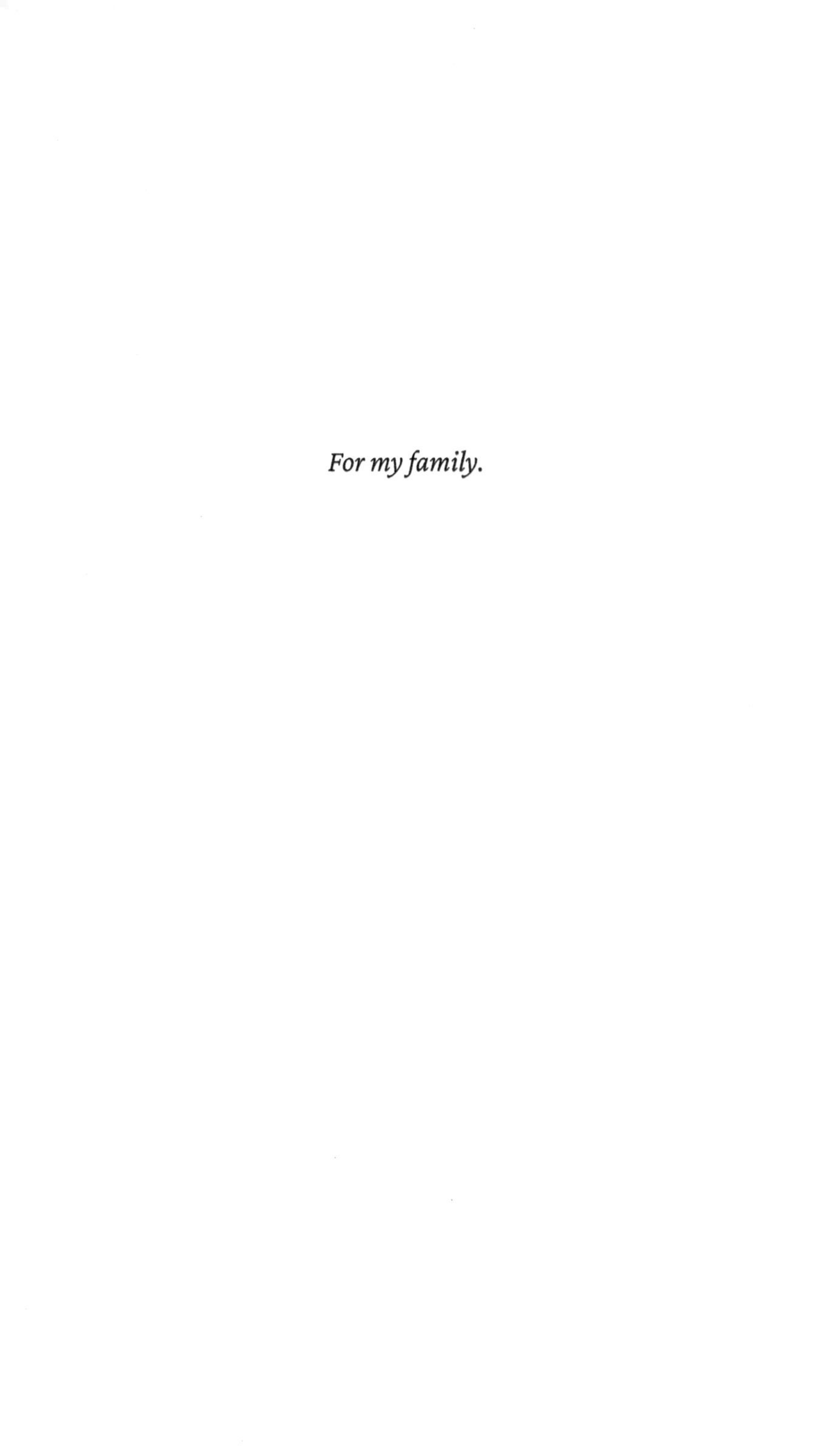

For my family.

Craving Stardust

Dad Bod Dragon

Mated to the Dragon

Jasmine's Grumpy Genie

Swamp Thing (You Make My Heart Sing)

You can find her books on Amazon.

ORC'S TAMING

I want to begin a new life far from my village. Will that life include an orc who vows to adore me?

Kaila: When a man in my village makes demands I'm not willing to give into, my younger brother and I flee into the forest. It's the night of the Monster Mate Hunt, but the orcs who are gifted with brides in exchange for protecting the village will be too busy with the other woman to notice me.

Until Turren claims me as his mate. I'm not interested in marrying, and orcs scare me. But there's something sweet and endearing about this one. My brother and I planned to make a new life far from our village. Could that new life be with Turren?

Turren: Kaila's fierce and strong-willed, and in no time, I can't imagine a world without her. In exchange for taking her and her brother to the new village on the edge of the forest, she agrees to let me woo her during our journey. And me, a male of very few words, has talked her into giving me three kisses. I'm going to do all I can to convince her we're destined to be together, even if that means speaking of feelings and my past, things I've shared with no one.

When we reach the village, will Kaila leave me, or will she agree to be my mate?

Orc's Taming is Book 5 in the Monster Mate Hunt Series. Expect a seductive orc hero with a creative. . . (cough), size difference, a fierce, scarred woman who will do anything to protect those she loves, plus a fantasy world you'll want to live in. HEA guaranteed. Each book is standalone, but the series is more fun if read in order.

Monster Mate Hunt
Books in Order:
Orc's Mate
(a prequel novel –
FREE with newsletter sign-up)
Orc's Craving
Orc's Fate

Orc's Maiden

Orc's Captive

Orc's Taming

FOREWORD

Monster Mate Hunt Terms, Characters, General Information

Orc's Mate (takes place 5 years before Orc's Craving):
Zephyr Clan: Air. Pendant is a circular disc made up of swirls to represent the air and water

Characters: Odik Brunellon, Eleri. Their children: Zur, Yusta

Birgid: woman who taunts Eleri and murdered Zur, the hunter who raised Eleri

Cassatine: orc midwife

Crikin: Dakur's father

Drabass: male from Odik's clan

Madine: elderly orc female; the keeper of clan stories

Trilden: Odik's friend

Zarran: Odik's vox

Zur: elderly man who adopted Eleri. They named their son after him

Orc's Craving, Book 1

Azuris Clan: Water/Sea. Pendant: metal swirls with spikes resembling waves

Characters: Rhoslyn, Jaus Kreedaull, Shirra: their daughter

Arkest: oldest, most revered healer

Eamon: village mayor who wants Rhoslyn for himself

Feyla: Jaus's female vox

Kael: older guardsman

King Surled: Jaus & Madr's father

Liall: older orc who runs an herb shop in the orc city

Lyneth: Rhoslyn's sister; married to Sveth

Mastivule: head of the kingdom's guards

Viskeete: rather crude orc

Orc's Fate, Book 2

Lumen Clan: sun/mountains. Pendant: shaped like the sun, it represents the mountains and the heavens above

Characters: Madr Thourand, Lyneth

Brakkis: Madr's vox

Finsteg: Matis Clan male who challenges Madr

Grock: Azuris clan male who guards Lyneth and is

murdered

Kael: older village guardsman, friend to Lyneth

Milllamay: shayde Dakur raised

Pulost: Matis Clan male who challenges Madr

Riank: Madr's cousin who wishes to rule

Sessavia: Matis Clan female, welcomes Lyneth

Taen: shayde Dakur raised

Tenkaril: Madr's mother, adopted Zickar; wise woman who "sees" when she touches someone

Tescall: Riank's younger brother and ally

Orc's Maiden, Book 3

Matis Clan: forest. Pendant: spikes from the sun like sunlight stabbing through the canopy

Characters: Zickar, Alwen, their son: Ferrin

Bredar: Alwen's brother

Brillie: Flazant female

Creea: Alwen's sister

Dillu: Flazant male

Loobek: orc male who went looking for Dakur

Mavileen: human woman, leader of the village on the edge of the forest

Nayleen: Alwen's sister

Noul: shayde Dakur raised

Pirrah: Flazant elder

Roolina: Alwen's mother

Rusket: older orc male

Trillie: Flazant female

Ulong: orc metal worker

Villadeer: Flazant female
Wambak: Flazant male

Orc's Captive, Book 4
Matis Clan
Characters: Dakur, Nia
Brunt: Nia's stepbrother
Kengart: head of Brunt's guards
Lianire: Brunt's second in command
Veegar: human male, cook
Woobedon: Nia's village built in the middle of the vast desert, near an oasis

Orc's Taming, Book 5
Ember Clan: desert/fire. Pendant: flames shooting toward the sky
Characters: Turren, Kaila

Vox history: Winged creatures fostered in the Ember Clan and bonded with orcs. They form within a seed and when they slip out, they bond with the person closest to them. In earlier days, this was their parent, but now all eligible males and females travel to the Ember Clan to be there for the hatching. The bonded orc remains with the hatchling long enough for the vox to grow for flight, feeding and grooming it so it knows their touch and smell. They nest near their bonded orc but return to the Ember territory every three years when they're ready to produce young.

General Terms:

Ashenclaw: creature like a wolf

Aspest berries: found on Odik's island, can be added to tea

Avestilar: large birds who nest high in the canopy

Brugel: meat like bacon

Caedos: leader of a clan

Chall: like a cat; kits are their young

Cheerish: type of bird

Clik: distance; about a mile

Daphoon: a dolphin-like sea creature

Doonet: a light cloth made from a plant

Dresalod: vicious, enormous crab-like sea creatures that attack the orc city

Elkern: timid creature like a deer

Effervast trees: fragrant

Fillawate: drink made from a rare fruit that grows deep beneath the ground. When fermented and drank, makes someone feel happy, though it's not alcohol

Flazant: stone people born of the boulders around us. Prior allies to the orcs

Hilardep: enormous, venomous spider found in the forest

Liladek flowers: lovely scent, bloom at night

Lindenmint: herb Rhoslyn drinks as tea; has antibacterial properties, slows a cut's blood flow. Found to be highly toxic to dresalods

Mellabar: a fruit jam

Orcling: orc baby/child

Reskit: creature like a rabbit

Ribber: creature like a rat

Secondist: Tuesday

Shayde: large, vicious, lizard-like creatures who live and hunt in the forest

Sinderfluff: material like silk

Squitt: creature like a squirrel

Succire: a sweet red berry

Tartledge Sea: vast, purple sea beyond the Orc Kingdom

Teegar: plants used to propel orcs to canopy platforms or take them below ground. Serve as elevators. Fed with diluted fillawate.

Teetser: a fly/mosquito

Trulist: trees that grow in thick groves

Wanderer: orc who travels, learning new ways to use their pendants

Weelen leaves: used in tea

Whisp: an insect that, when blown across, lights up. Used in lanterns as a source of light

Willadon: a black root, made into a tea that relieves arthritis pain

CHAPTER 1

KAILA

"Your boss told me to come find you," my younger brother, Brunnen, said. "He said he wants to speak with you."

My sigh slipped out of me. I couldn't hold it back. Straightening from where I was weeding the village's vegetable garden, I turned to face Brunnen. I'd raised him since our parents died ten years ago when he was three and I was twelve, and there wasn't anyone I loved more than him.

I only kept this job because it came with a tiny house and my boss, Jabon, allowed Brunnen to stay there with me.

Sunlight highlighted Brunnen's black hair much like my own, and the sorrow in his green eyes we also shared hit me like a knife in the chest. He yanked on his shirt, and I pinched my eyes closed to shut out the sight of how the worn fabric outlined his thin frame. I worked incredibly hard, and I was allowed to take home the vegetables that had begun to spoil, but there was just never quite enough to sustain us both.

I was never enough.

"Did he say why he wants to talk with me?" I really didn't need to ask. He'd told me I must give him my answer by the end of today. *Answer?* He'd made a demand, and I told him I needed time to think about it. Because others were near enough to hear if I called out for help, he'd reluctantly agreed to my request.

Few would've rushed to my aid. We all needed our jobs, and Jabon could do what he pleased. Only Brunnen would've come over and socked Jabon. The last thing I wanted was for my young brother to attack my boss. He'd fire me, and we'd be homeless.

Slanting a quick look around, Brunnen lowered his voice. "We need to run, Kaila. I told you I've been saving. We can go to another village. I hear there's one on the other side of the forest run by women. If we ask the leader of that village nicely, she might let me live there with you. They'll take you in for sure. You're smart and plants sprout up just to stand in your light."

I stroked his cheek. "You're sweet to say that." A blush bloomed on his face, and he huffed, but I knew he still craved affection as much as me. "How much money do you have?" I was more curious than excited. A few pennies would not be enough to begin a new life.

I was beginning to resign myself to the fact that I'd have to tell Jabon yes.

Brunnen tugged some coins from his pocket and held them out to me. So few. The color deepened in his face, telling me he was incredibly proud of what he'd collected.

"Where did you get them?" A thread of fear shot through me. Brunnen was sweet and innocent. It would be easy for someone to take advantage of him.

Stiffening his spine, he stood tall, towering over me, but I was tiny for a village woman. "I earned them. The smithy allows me to watch, and a few times, he's let me load wood into the burner or brace a particularly long piece of metal. He said if I'm diligent and fast, he might take me on as an apprentice soon."

"That would be wonderful." The apprenticeship would come with room and board.

He'd have no place with me if I agreed to Jabon's demands.

"Is this enough for us to run?" Hope clung to his words and in his eyes. I hated to crush his dream, but we'd need a lot more than that to outfit us for a long journey through the forest.

"Maybe." I nibbled on my lower lip. "I have a bit saved myself." Perhaps we *could* run. The Monster Mate Hunt would be held tonight, and in the furor, we might be able to slip from the fortress and race in the opposite direction. We'd find a place to hide until morning. After the orcs had claimed their brides, something they did annually in exchange for providing us protection from the shaydes, Brunnen and I could make our way through the woods to the village he'd mentioned.

I'd heard women had left other villages, tired of being told what to do and given no freedom. They'd built a new home and ran things themselves, only taking husbands if they pleased.

No one made demands of them they weren't willing to fill. What would that be like?

"Kaila!"

Brunnen and I both jolted when Jabon bellowed my name.

I swallowed hard and tucked strands of my long hair behind my ear. They'd worked their way out of my braid. I was sweaty, sunburned, and dirt covered my clothing and face.

And yet, my boss would still want me.

"I'll go to him," I said softly. "I'll find a way to make him wait a little bit longer. That'll give us more time."

"I'm coming with you." My brother's lower lip trembled, but his eyes took on the flinty slant I remembered from our strong father who'd died trying to protect our mother, succumbing along with her. Brunnen might be slight and small for his age, but he was as fierce as me.

If he confronted my boss, he'd be in grave danger.

I gave Brunnen a pleasant smile, though I had to

work hard to maintain it. "There's no need to come with me. Why don't you go home? Heat the soup I made for us last night. I'll be there soon, and we can eat it together." My belly rumbled at the thought of finally putting something in it other than water and a few raw vegetables.

Brunnen studied my face for a long while before jerking out a nod. "I don't like him. Not one bit."

It was funny how children could see right through a person to the evil festering inside.

I nudged his side. "Go. I won't be long."

After staring at me for a heartbeat, he turned and stomped down the row of beans and onto the main path winding through the big garden area. When he reached Jabon waiting, he paused, but after sending me a sad look, he continued past my boss and through the open gate beyond. Our small home was on the right, the last in a row of buildings offered to those who'd worked here the longest. I'd been employed in the fields for ten years.

I gathered my basket holding my water jug and the wrapper that had held the vegetables I'd eaten for lunch and walked toward Jabon. No one stood near him, unfortunately, so I wasn't sure I could use the pressure of others overhearing to get him to change his mind. He'd already given me an ultimatum, and I doubted I could stretch it much farther.

"It's time, Kaila," he said when I reached him, latching onto my upper arm. He pivoted and marched toward the central building where some ate their lunch, dragging me behind him. Everyone was either still working in the field or they'd left for the day. We rotated shifts to ensure someone was working in the gardens from before the sun rose until well past sunset. I'd worked the middle shift today.

Inside his office, he shut the door and pressed me against it, caging me with his palms on either side of my head.

I scooted beneath his arm and around his desk to put space between us. The open window behind could provide a route of escape, though there was no permanent way to avoid him forever, not if I wanted to hold on to this job.

"You agree?" he asked in a deadly voice.

"I need more time to decide."

He sighed. "There's no decision to make. You'll warm my bed, or you'll find another job."

"It's not fair. I'll tell the mayor."

"My brother?" He released a low laugh. "Do you truly think he'll protect you from me?"

"I pay taxes like everyone else." I stiffened my spine. "I'm entitled to have protection as much as the next person."

"You don't need protection from me."

Yes, I did. "Give me two more days, and I promise I'll . . ." I pinched my eyes closed, but I didn't keep them that way before snapping them open. No need to give him time to leap. "Then I'll come to your bed."

He grumbled but surely, he wanted me willing?

"Alright." He watched me, so I gave him a smile. "Two days, but no longer than that." His slick smile rose. "I'll be sure to change my sheets that day."

When he left, I wanted to collapse in his chair, but there was no way I'd remain in his territory. I scooted out the door, and spying him walking out into the field to speak with a different worker, I rushed to the right. I hurried home and shut the door, leaning against it while trying not to shriek.

"The soup's almost ready," Brunnen said, waving to the small table. He'd picked some wildflowers and propped the stems in a mug. "Sit. You worked hard today in the sun."

"You're the best person in the world." It was all I could do not to blubber. Tension spiraled inside me, but it was too late to think of any other way out of this but one.

"So are you, Kaila." He came over and hugged me, something he hadn't done for months, not since he turned thirteen. *I've grown up too much for that,* he'd said. *You understand.*

I did, but I missed being close to him. When he was little, he'd snuggle on my lap, falling asleep in my arms.

We sat and ate, and after, I leaned back in my chair, giving him a steady look. "I . . ." I hated to tear him from the only home he'd known, but we had no choice. My brother wouldn't survive here without me.

And I couldn't bear the thought of lying beneath Jabon while he rutted.

"You're right," I said. "We need to run."

Brunnen nodded, his eyes widening.

"Let's combine our coins and go buy provisions." Rising, I took my bowl to the counter. Normally, I'd wash it in the central area. We had no running water in our home. After, I'd return it to the cupboard and tidy the small kitchen. We'd sit in the adjacent area, talking about general things or telling each other stories. Sometimes, we played a game we'd made up with sticks and smooth pebbles.

Not tonight.

"We'll pack our things," I said, turning to lean against the counter. "Tonight, we'll leave the village forever."

CHAPTER 2

TURREN

Along with thirty or so other orcs, I crouched on a thick branch high in the canopy, waiting for two women to leave the human fortress. Because my clan lived so far from here, I'd never participated in the Monster Mate Hunt. I was attending this year only because I'd recently traveled with Dakur, the caedos of the Matis Clan. He'd been captured and trapped far out in the desert where my clan made their home, and I'd helped him and his new mate, Nia. He'd invited me to stay with him before the Hunt.

One of the other orcs studied me, his gaze falling on my left arm.

Keeping my face stoic, I tucked it against my side to hide the scars, to keep him from noting it was slighter than my right.

He said nothing, but none of us wanted to make a

sound that might call in predators who'd hunt the women.

It wasn't hard for me to remain silent. I was known for saying very little. When I did speak, I tried to craft my words in a way that gave them meaning.

The canopy rustled overhead, and I peered up, tightening my grip on the blade sheathed at my waist.

I hated it here, hate being perhaps too strong a word. I missed the wide-open spaces surrounding my home, the dry air, the endless sunshine, and the creatures we rode in the sky. There, I could see for many cliks in every direction. I knew how to find food and water. No one found me lacking.

Deep within the forest, I could barely see beyond the length of my arms. It was damp here, and I didn't understand the sounds creatures and insects made. I didn't know how to protect myself from whatever might stalk me.

With that in mind, I tapped the hilt of my staff sheathed along my spine. I could pull it in a blink, and with it in my hands, there were few who could defeat me in battle.

"One comes," the male beside me wearing a Matis Clan pendant whispered, pointing toward the high fortress gate that was creaking open. "It's said they fight us, that they don't wish to become our brides, but I'm not sure I believe that. Look at how Alwen adores Zickar, how Nia can't bear to be out of Dakur's sight." He scoffed. "If the fates are kind enough to send me my fated one tonight, she'll welcome me with wide open arms." His smile bloomed. "And I'll adore her for the rest of my days. What do you think?"

"I . . ."

He leaned closer to hear my soft words.

I cleared my throat. "I think I'll be eternally grateful if the fates treat me kindly tonight."

While I'd found a new home with my clan, and I had many friends, I was lonely. Would a human woman be able to fill the hole in my heart?

A woman crept through the open gate, a bag clutched in her hand and a stoic expression on her pretty face. Her long silver hair tied high on her head gleamed in the moonlight, the light displaying her lush form.

Light blazed nearby, and a male perched on a tree limb a few trees over from mine groaned. He grinned and looked down at his Azuris pendant that was made up of swirls with spikes to resemble waves. I hadn't seen the ocean, and I wasn't sure I ever would. The oases where my clan lived in the summer months contained pools that were big enough for me.

"Go," a male said, slapping the back of the Azuris clansmale with the blazing pendant. "Your clan fates have chosen her for you. Now, you only need to claim her. She waits for you."

"She looks more like she's running away from him," someone else said with a low laugh, pointing to where the female had entered the woods and was fleeing down a weaving trail into the darkness beyond. "Perhaps she wishes for you to capture her before you announce your intentions?"

With a rueful shake of his head, the chosen male leaped all the way to the ground, landing with a dull thud, and took off after her.

The rest of the orcs waiting in the canopy sighed with envy.

Another woman left the fortress, and the door banged closed. No more women would leave the fortress tonight, and the next hunt would not take place for another year. As part of the treaty between the orcs and the humans, the orcs provided protection from the forest creatures in exchange for two mates.

The Matis Pendant hanging around the neck of the male next to me flamed, and he shot me a grin before jumping to the ground and rushing over to meet her as she entered the woods. She cried out with joy or dismay—I couldn't tell. He took her hand and disappeared with her into the dense vegetation.

"Another year to wait," someone said, and the others grumbled, me included. This was a wasted trip. I wouldn't come to the hunt again.

Then my pendant flared, blazing so brightly, it blinded me for a heartbeat. Everyone turned to look my way.

"Three?" someone said in awe.

Another grunted. "It's not possible. The treaty states we only get two."

"Where is she?" another asked, peering around.

I looked too. The fortress gate remained closed. No woman walked through the woods around us, and I didn't hear any movement other than from the other males.

"Are the fates mistaken?" someone asked.

That wasn't possible. She was out there somewhere, and I was going to find her.

I sprung from the branch, landing solidly on the crushed leaves coating the ground and lifted my head. Could I scent her?

Yes . . . I caught a light floral essence to the north that called to me like no other. It stabbed through my heart that longed to find my other perfect half.

I burst into a run, determined to claim her in the name of the Ember Clan.

CHAPTER 3
KAILA

Nothing had gone right tonight. The merchants had refused to bargain for supplies, and what little we'd been able to purchase with our precious coins wouldn't last us for more than a day or two. We had many days of travel through the forest before we'd reach the village settled by women on the other side.

And tonight was the Hunt. Wasn't that the way of the world?

If we could make it safely out of the village, I would have to do all I could to avoid being claimed as an orc's bride.

Moonlight whispered across the ground, lighting the way as Brunnen and I crept across the village to the fortress wall. A guard paced on the top, and we waited in the shadows until he'd rounded a corner and continued, his gaze focused on the woods.

We'd purposefully chosen the gate on the opposite side of the fortress from where women would be sent out for the Hunt.

Waiting, we said nothing, not wanting to draw attention, using only hand signals to indicate when it was time for us to approach the back gate.

A guard stood beside it, yawning and shuffling his feet.

We remained where we were, hoping our opportunity would come quickly.

Sweat coiled down my spine, and I shifted in my boots, wishing I'd changed into pants and wasn't wearing my usual long skirt and loose blouse.

Finally, the guard grunted and made his way across the open area between the fortress wall and the guardhouse, going inside.

This was our chance. With a wave of my hand, we sprinted toward the gate. It opened easily, though it creaked like an old man's bones. We froze, but when no one called out, we slipped through the opening and shut it carefully behind us.

Then we raced across the open field toward the woods, quickly finding shelter among the trees.

CHAPTER 4
TURREN

I heard my mate before I saw her. While my clan pendant flared intermittently, reminding me it had chosen her for me, I didn't need the pendant to tell me she was near.

I also *sensed* her, as if she stroked her soft hands on my body. I could taste the heat of her kiss, and the way she'd melt against my frame. As it had been for all orcs before me, so it would be between my mate and me. From our first meeting, I'd adore her. If she didn't feel the same for me immediately, it wouldn't take long. So the fates decreed.

I only needed to claim her in the name of my clan, and she'd welcome me into her arms.

A rustling in the forest ahead showed me where she was, and with my staff held tight in my hand, I eased forward, making no sound. When I saw her highlighted by a stab of moonlight, my breathing came to a shuddering halt. I remained in place, watching her, caressing her lush frame with my eyes.

She was lovely with her long black hair flowing out behind her and the way she plucked her way carefully through the woods.

Would I be able to find the words to tell her the feelings growing in my heart? Perhaps, with her, I'd finally find my voice.

With a grin on my face, I rushed toward her, striding from the woods and across the small open area, not stopping until I stood right in front of her.

She yelped and reeled away, gaping up at me with complete shock.

"Lovely mate," I rasped, my heart roaring and my pulse on fire. Words. I'd found the words! "I am Turren Dhivair. I claim you in the name of the Ember Clan." I took her hand, and warmth flowed up my arm, centering in my groin. My cock responded beneath my loincloth, expanding, thickening with hot blood. "Will you tell me your name?"

She shrieked and wrenched her hand from mine, backing from me. If her gaze hadn't shot past me, alerting me that someone else was near, the glancing blow of a stick would've hit me squarely in the back of my head instead of on my shoulder.

"Go away," a male cried.

I whirled, determined to protect my mate at all costs, and lifted my staff.

A male stood nearby. He was too lean, but the

strong threat in his green eyes told me he'd do all he could to defend himself. "Don't touch her."

Did this puny specimen think he could steal my mate from me?

Never.

With a growl, I leaped on him, bringing him quickly to the ground.

He cried out and flailed, smacking me with a stick until I yanked it from his grip and tossed it aside. I grabbed his hands in one of mine and pinned them to the ground on either side of his head.

"Do you die now, or do you relent?" I snarled.

"Leave him alone." My mate hurled herself on top of me like an ashenclaw defending its young. I shrugged her off, though I snapped my arm out to slow her fall. She landed on the ground on her side and sprung to her feet, tears streaming down her face. "Get away from my brother you . . . you fiend!"

"I'm your mate," I said softly, puzzled by her response. Didn't she adore me like I did her already?

And did she say brother? I looked between them, taking in the similar features, the same hair and eye color.

This was a youngling, not a puny man.

Releasing him, I levered myself up and off him, stepping back while he sat up and groaned, rubbing the back of his head.

My mate flung herself in front of him, baring her

teeth at me. "Leave us alone. I'm not your mate. I'm not anyone's mate!"

"My pendant . . ." On cue, it flared brightly, something it would do until I'd fully claimed her supposedly willing body. That was what the legends said, that she'd love me like no other until the day I died, that I'd feel the same. Already, I felt a pull toward her. I wanted to scoop her up, spin around with her in my arms, and kiss her. Nuzzle her throat while I roamed my hands across her sweet body.

However, she did not appear to feel the same way, and that . . . hurt. I ignored the sadness crushing my throat and stepped back a few paces while her brother rose and thrust her behind him.

"My pendant blazes only for you, my precious one," I said softly, hoping I could somehow, in some way, convince her of the feelings blooming in my heart. Where were my words now that I needed them most? "We're mates."

"You need to leave," she said bitterly. "We're fleeing the village, not participating in the Hunt. We don't want or need you around."

"I cannot leave you." I struggled to share my feelings that were full of life and hope. "I am tethered to you for the rest of my days."

That . . . didn't sound good enough, but I couldn't think of anything else to say.

When she crossed her arms on her chest, her

breasts swelled upward, the tops straining above her blouse. "Well, then, I feel bad for you, because frankly, being tethered to anyone sucks." Squinting, she lifted her hand to shield her face. "Make that thing stop glowing, would you? Shaydes will see it from cliks away and race toward us to attack."

I cupped my pendant, cursing it, though only for a blink of an eye. "It will stop shining . . ." With a sigh, I didn't name it. She clearly didn't want to hear, didn't want to listen.

Didn't want me.

I felt adrift, lost in the buffeting sands stirred up by a storm in my desert home. What future did I have if my mate rejected me? I would still be caedos. My clan would still welcome me among them as such. But for the rest of my life, I'd feel as if someone has sliced me wide open, cutting away a part of me and tossing it aside.

I'd *bleed*.

"You said," I swallowed and made myself speak. "You're fleeing the village?" I latched onto that one statement.

The youngling lifted his chin. "We're going to the women's village on the other side of the forest. We'll find a welcome there."

"You'd find a welcome with my clan." I had to point it out.

"Where's that?" he asked, frowning.

"Far beyond the forest, in the desert."

He scoffed. "I've heard of the desert, how it's a torturous place filled with endless sand, wind, and heat that bakes you like clay in the sunlight. How you'll quickly get lost and starve there. You'll dry out when you discover there's no water to be found."

"There *is* water there. Life." Pinching my eyes closed, I tried to think of what might convince them —*her*. "There's incredible beauty in the desert." A beauty I feared my mate would never see. "As for the women's village, I've been there."

Excitement bloomed in the youngling's eyes. "You have?"

My mate watched us, saying nothing, her gaze sliding down my frame without the devotion I craved more than I needed to breathe.

"Yes, it's to the west of here," I said.

The youngling looked to the east.

"And the orc kingdom is that way, by the sea," I said, still watching every move my mate made. Did she realize how her eyes warmed when she looked at her brother, how they hardened to a green darker than the rare emerst stone we sometimes found in caverns deep in the mountains? How her feet shifted, and she actually took a step toward me? She must, because her eyes widened with shock, and she moved back to stand behind her brother again.

"Which way is west?" the youngling asked.

"What's your name? What's your sister's name?"

"Don't—"

He cut her off. "I'm Brunnen. She's Kaila."

"Brunnen," she groaned, peering past his shoulder at me. "You shouldn't tell this orc anything. He'll use it against you."

"So far, well, other than knocking me to the ground and pinning my hands, he's been decent," Brunnen said. "Maybe those horrible stories about orcs actually are lies. Maybe the ones we heard whispered by those who'd talked with the women who mated with orcs in the past are the real truth." He stepped to the side, revealing her watching me, her limbs quivering. She looked ready to bolt, only holding herself back because she didn't know in which direction to run.

"As I said, the women's village is to the west. The desert's to the south." When it came to topics such as this, it wasn't hard to speak.

"Thanks." The youngling stalked over and grabbed the bag he dropped when he attacked me. He hefted the stick as well, holding it in a way that told me he'd one day be quite formidable—with the proper training. "Let's go, Kaila."

"You must travel during the day and find shelter at night," I called out to them.

Far in the distance, a shayde's chitter rang out.

Kaila and Brunnen froze.

I walked over to stand beside her. "If you travel at night, the shaydes and ashenclaws will hunt you. They scent prey from many cliks."

"Yet you orcs hold the mate hunt at night," she said dryly.

I hefted my staff. "We easily fight them off." I wasn't bragging. This was true.

Brunnen's hand tightened on his stick, but his hand shook. He shot me a wild look of panic, and my heart ached for the youngling. He was brave, and he'd do his best to protect his sister, but in this, they were mere orclings.

"It's also three days' travel through the dense forest to the women's village," I said softly. "Do you have provisions?"

Kaila's gaze shot to the limp bag that appeared to hold a paltry number of possessions. "We have enough."

"Water?"

With her chin lifting, her emerst eyes met mine. "We'll remain close to the river."

"I can hunt," the youngling said. "I'll set traps. I've done it before."

"I can tell you'll be a strong warrior one day," I said. The youngling puffed his chest and shot his sister a smug look. "You'll provide well for your future mate and young."

"I will," he said eagerly. "Do you hunt?"

"I'm caedos." I named this to show my mate I had worth. Despite all that had happened to me, my clan saw my value even if my family never had. When Brunnen's face creased with confusion, I explained. "I'm the leader of my clan, and yes, I hunt. We all do."

"*Even* leaders?" the boy asked. "Why? Don't you have . . . leadership things to do?" He looked again at his sister. "Our mayor doesn't do a damn thing. He lets everyone else do it for him. I bet Turren's a good leader." Admiration shone in his voice.

"I try my best. None of my people have voiced complaints."

Kaila huffed, her fingers flexing at her sides. "I'm sure the mayor says the same thing."

"A good leader doesn't need to brag."

"And yet you did."

Because I was savoring her fiery spirit, my lips coiled up. "If you meet them, you can ask them yourself."

My words were . . . coming easier. Perhaps because this was my mate and my soul recognized what she still denied?

"We know that will never happen," she said. "Come on, Brunnen. We need to get going."

Was there a way to persuade my mate to remain with me for now?

Yes, there was. "I assume you two will find your way to the village eventually, assuming . . ."

They both watched me intently, the boy with a touch of hope and my mate with complete scorn.

"Assuming what?" she finally asked.

"Assuming you can fight off the shaydes."

As if to punctuate my words, another chitter echoed in the deep woods, much closer now than before.

CHAPTER 5
KAILA

My knees shook, and my pulse fluttered behind my ribcage. I could already feel the shayde's claws sinking into my spine, its fangs ripping out my throat.

The orc—Turren—turned on his heel and started across the tiny meadow.

My brother took a step after him. "Wait."

"Brunnen," I hissed. When Turren turned, I flicked my hand toward him. "Keep going. Goodbye." I resisted the urge to sarcastically call him *mate*. What kind of fool did he take me for? A pendant couldn't magically pick someone to marry.

He wasn't mine, and I would never be his.

"Maybe this orc can help us," Brunnen pleaded low by my ear. "At least stay with us tonight. We'll travel during the day tomorrow like he suggests and sleep at night. A few days isn't a long time."

"I could take you there," Turren said.

Brunnen's eyes lit up. I put a restraining hand on his arm before he bounded over to the orc like a chall in love with a new master.

"We can get there on our own," I insisted. "We don't need his help."

"I was merely offering." Turren's eyes remained locked on mine, not traveling down my frame in a greedy way like Jabon. "When we get there, I could introduce you to Mavileen, the caedos of the village."

"We don't need you," I pretty much shouted.

A bellow rang out from my right and dull thuds echoed, coming in this direction.

"Yes, I can see that," Turren said with a soft laugh, an infernal sound that raked down my spine like a beast's claws. "You'll do very well on your own."

"Kaila," Brunnen whined, shifting his feet in the thick grass.

"I can hunt while we travel," Turren said, as if this added incentive would make *all* the difference. "Show you the safest places to drink from the river, where to sleep at night, and . . ." The words rushed out of him, seeming to surprise even him. Wasn't he used to talking? "And you'll have the might of my staff as we travel." He hefted it again, displaying the chiseled, sharp tip on the end, the thickness of its shaft. Muscles on his chest, arms, and abdomen rippled with the movement beneath his medium-green skin. Except . . .

Only now did I note that his left arm was not only

covered with thick scars, but it also looked slightly smaller than the right. What kind of injury had he sustained to do that much damage?

For one moment, I felt sympathy for this orc.

"Why would you want to do something like this for us?" I asked. There was always a price.

What would he want in exchange for his help? As I watched him, a warm feeling bloomed low in my belly. He was attractive—for an orc. The warmth was merely my natural response to such a formidable male. Like many women, I found strength and a strong will appealing in a visceral way. We were all drawn to someone who made it clear they could protect us.

"I'm sure we can come to . . ." He swallowed, his gaze drifting to the ground. "Some sort of agreement."

Something was crashing in the woods, coming this way. We didn't have time for negotiations. It was all I could do not to bolt in the opposite direction.

Brunnen nodded raptly, oblivious to the hunting beast. I wanted to snarl at him, but he was the youngling Turren had named him. At thirteen, he did his best to help and be there for me, but he had some growing to do before he could step into a man's shoes.

Turren appeared to fill them well already.

"What are you suggesting?" I asked.

His lips flickered upward, and moonlight snagged on his white tusks almost as long as my smallest finger. What would it be like to kiss a male with tusks? I bet they'd press into my skin. Hurt.

He stood proudly before us, practically naked, something unheard of in the village where men wore thick trousers and long-sleeved shirts even in the heat of the summer, the latter to protect their skin from biting teetsers. His simple loincloth merely enhanced his gorgeous physique. As for his arm, it actually made him appear . . . braver. As if he'd survived something horrible and come out the other side a better male for all the suffering.

His loincloth barely covered the sizeable bulge between his legs that stirred at my attention.

I huffed. He was just like all males, thinking of only one thing—a thing they'd be glad to take, never woo from a woman. Was it too much to ask for a male to defer to her in something like this even once?

"Here's my offer," he said in a low voice that tickled across my skin. He frowned toward the woods where the beast crashed around.

I didn't like feeling attracted to him. Didn't like him.

"I'll take you to the village," he said softly, his hand tightening on his wooden shaft. "We'll travel during the day, and I'll provide your food. I'll protect you from threats, and you'll be able to sleep soundly without fear of being attacked. I'll even bring you to the tops of the trees at night to rest."

"Why the tops of the trees?" Brunnen asked eagerly, shooting me a look that told me my poor brother so eager for a father figure had found one in an orc we randomly met in the forest.

"Shaydes and ashenclaws can't climb," Turren said quite seriously.

"Won't we fall?"

"Not if you rest on a wide branch."

"What other conditions?" I snarled, breaking through their male bonding. I shifted toward him, my skin crawling with fear that whatever was in the woods nearby would attack. "You're not offering to do this out of the goodness of your heart."

Turren's lips curled up on one side.

My heart flipped over.

"What if I was?" he asked.

"What do you want?" I bit out.

His golden eyes met mine. "I'll do all this for you . . ."

And here it is. There was always *something*.

"As long as you let me woo you."

CHAPTER 6
TURREN

It seemed that in my desperation to convince Kaila we were true mates; I'd come up with the plan. The beast crashing through the woods gave me aid.

Didn't she know? There was no way I'd leave her and her brother to make their own way to a village three days' travel from here with predators stalking them. If she insisted they do this alone, I'd shadow them, remaining far enough behind they wouldn't know I was there but close enough to protect them.

"Woo me?" she barked.

Brunnen shot a panicked glance toward the forest. "Kaila. Stop shouting. We're going to get eaten by shaydes and it'll be your fault."

She whirled to face her brother. "We don't need him. And I don't need him trying to get me into his bed."

"There are no beds in the forest," I kindly pointed out.

"You know what I mean. I'm not having sex with you."

Brunnen sighed and turned toward her. After lowering his stick to the ground, he braced her upper arms, holding her still, looking down at her. "I love you, Kaila."

"I love you too, Brunnen."

"I'd do anything for you."

"Same."

"If you say traveling alone is something we must do, then I'll follow. I'll do my best to hunt, and I'll stay awake all night to protect you. I'll even fight off the beast coming this way."

"Brunnen," she half-wailed. "I don't want to have sex with him."

He growled and shot me a look that again told me that this male would be a strong warrior one day. "No sex."

"I'd never force her to do anything she didn't want to," I said.

Brunnen turned back to Kaila. "I can't do everything." The starkness in his voice cut through my chest, leaving me bleeding.

It must've done the same thing to my mate because she staggered.

His hands on her arms shored her up. "Our odds of

surviving this journey go up substantially if we're with Turren."

"No . . ."

"I want you to listen to what he has to offer." Again, he looked my way, as if he needed to state this once more. "No sex."

"I'd never force her to have sex with me." No orc would ever make a woman do something like that.

Brunnen grunted and turned back to Kaila. "You two need to work this out. I'm going to walk in the opposite direction of that beast. I'll stay close enough to hear you if you shout. But you two need to determine where we go from here." he released her and stalked to the forest, easing among the trees before stopping. I could still see him, but he was right that he probably couldn't hear us.

"No sex," Kaila snarled at me.

"Not unless you want it."

"Well, I can comfortably state that I never will."

"Instead . . ." I couldn't believe I was able to think around her, let alone speak. Fortunately, whatever was in the woods didn't seem to be coming this way anymore. Perhaps it was a large herbivore and not a predator picking up our scent.

"Instead what?"

"I . . ." If there was ever a time to speak, it was now. "I also want three kisses and for you to rest with me at night." A daring move on my part. "They're part of the wooing."

"There you go again. If I rest with you at night, you'll take advantage of me."

"I told you I wouldn't. My word is my vow."

She studied me a long time before jerking out a nod. "What exactly does orc wooing entail?" At least she wasn't outright refusing my kisses or resting with me.

"I'll care for you, show you complete devotion. I'll . . . try to talk to you."

"You're talking now."

"I'm a male of few words most of the time."

"Except now," she said wryly.

"This is not usual for me."

She frowned. "I see." Her chin lifted. "What else?"

"I'll keep you safe and protect you."

"This sounds like something a parent would do."

My offer was much different from that of a parent, but she'd see.

"I don't like this," she said.

And I didn't want to force her, but I was desperate. If she walked away, yes, I'd follow. But this . . . this was a chance to show her how strong a mate bond could be. A chance to prove to her that I was worthy of love.

I waited patiently while emotions flitted across her face. Anger. Frustration. And finally, reluctant agreement.

"Alright," she said. "You have the three days it'll take to reach the village. Please know that no matter how much wooing you do, it won't make a difference.

I'm going to remain in the new village with my brother, and you're going to walk away."

We'd see about that.

"Good." I gave her a nod.

"I suppose you want a kiss now." Her lips twisted in disgust. "To solidify this cursed deal."

Inside, I quivered. Outside, I continued to show strength. But everywhere, I felt fear that it wouldn't matter what I did, that she'd reject me like everyone else other than my clan had.

"I don't want a kiss yet. I'll let you know when the time's right."

She rolled her eyes and softly called out to her brother, who strode back to join us. He looked back and forth from her to me. "All set?"

"Yes," she groaned.

I lifted my pendant and gently sent spurts of air across it, creating a series of low hums that would tell my vox waiting in the canopy above that he was to fly to the edge of the desert and wait. He'd eat and relax, waiting there for me patiently.

Kaila watched me with confusion on her face but said nothing.

Whatever was in the woods had moved on. I didn't hear shaydes coming near either. I could take a moment to show them what I had to offer.

I removed my pouch from where I'd strapped it to my lower back and opened it, giving them each a seed and dried fruit cake. We'd wash it down with water from my small flask, and it would tide us over until morning.

Afterward, I looked around and found a few likely trees. "I'll take Brunnen up to the canopy and then you, my . . . surly mate . . ."

She lifted one eyebrow.

"Then you, mate, will climb a tree with me."

CHAPTER 7
KAILA

"I need to . . ." Cringing, I started walking toward the bushes.

He followed.

"I won't run," I barked. "You don't need to go with me."

His lips twitching upward before smoothing, and he lifted his staff. "I'll protect you, my fierce mate."

"Don't call me that."

"Fierce?"

I scowled. "I'm not your mate yet."

"Yet." His eyes sparkled, and my heart did a little dance.

I pressed my hand against my chest, hoping it would stop sashaying around. "I didn't mean yet."

"You said it." He waved his spear toward the woods. "Let's go, my soon-to-be-mate. You can take care of your needs, and I'll stand guard."

"I'm not letting you watch me pee."

"Kaila," Brunnen groaned, reminding me that he'd lost his patience with our squabbling already. "Please."

I huffed at Turren. "You can come with me, but you have to keep your back turned toward me."

He dipped his head forward. "I promise."

With a roll of my eyes, I stepped into the forest and walked enough distance from Brunnen that he wouldn't hear me taking care of my needs.

"Go back and protect my brother," I hissed.

"I will once you've finished." He frowned a second as if trying to find the right words, though I wasn't sure why I thought that. "The longer you take," his face cleared, "the longer he remains unprotected."

I wanted to howl. Instead, I hitched up my skirt, squatted, and relieved myself, swiping a leave I plucked from a nearby bush across that area once I'd finished. After straightening my clothing, I hurried back to my brother who'd sat on the grass with his legs stretched out, still nibbling on the meal Turren gave him.

He stood when we approached and tipped his head back, peering at the tall trees around us. "Are you sure we need to sleep up there?"

Turren nodded. With a grunt that must be his way of voicing a command, he walked into the woods again, following a path for some distance while looking up at the canopy. We followed.

When he stopped, he waved to my brother. "Up."

Brunnen basically galloped over to join him. If he had a tail, it would be wagging. Leave it to my brother to fall for Turren's charms from the moment he met him. I, a bit savvier, had not.

"How do I get up there?" my brother asked.

"I'll give you the initial boost and join you on the lowest branch. We'll make our way higher together and then I'll show you how mature orclings rest in the trees."

"Orclings like me do this all the time?"

"Those who live in the forest. My clan made their home in the desert and mountains beyond many generations ago."

"I've heard there are no trees in the desert," I said, reluctantly joining them at the base of the tree. Would I have to climb as well?

"There are not, but we don't need trees." He boosted Brunnen and then leaped, joining my brother as he straightened and looked upward. In a short time, they'd disappeared from view, and I no longer heard them moving above.

I jumped when Turren landed on the ground beside me, his tusks flashing in the moonlight once more.

"Do you smile all the time?" I asked, my mouth tasting sour.

"An interesting question."

"With you not giving me an answer."

"I . . . I don't speak a lot."

"You seem to be talking enough for me."

He smiled again. "I believe I'm able to find my words because you're my lovely mate."

I sighed, not wanting to go through that once more.

He nudged his head to the right, and I followed him through the woods. At least the beast we'd heard hadn't come near. Would Turren truly be able to fight off a ferocious creature? Yes, he had a staff. An enormous frame coated with rippling muscles. Strong legs and thick thighs.

I dragged my gaze away from his ass shifting smoothly beneath his loincloth as he moved ahead of me.

He paused, and before I could think or utter a sound, his hands spanned my waist, and he tossed me over his shoulder.

I yelped and smacked my palms on his back as he sprung upward, landing squarely on a branch.

"Don't wiggle," he said, peering upward.

"Put me down."

"Can you climb on your own?"

"Brunnen did."

"Your brother took my guidance. What about you, my amazing mate?"

"What's with all the descriptors?"

"As I said, around you, I'm finding my words."

He made no sense.

"I can listen well enough," I said.

He slid me much too slowly down his front and held me against his body while he gently placed my feet on the wide branch.

His cock pressed against me, and I gasped, trying to reel away. Before I could impact with the tree truck, he'd tugged me back into his arms.

"Take care, my gorgeous mate."

"Unhand me." I sounded like a ninety-year-old village virgin being accosted by a rogue while shopping in the market, but I couldn't help it. This male unbalanced me in too many ways.

"If I let go, do you promise not to flail and hit your precious body against the tree?" he asked in much too reasonable a tone, as if he was speaking to an unruly toddler.

"Tell me how to do this." I struggled not to sound like that toddler—or the old lady.

"Reach up. Grab the branch above. Use your feet to climb up onto the branch. Once there, repeat the step. Come. Do this. I'll follow. I'll also remain below you to catch you when you fall."

"I'm not going to fall." How hard could it be to climb a tree? Children in the village did it all the time.

Looking up, I spied a likely branch not far over my head and jumped, grateful when my arms locked around it, and I didn't plunge onto my ass. With fierce concentration, I studied the bark on the tree and placed my toes in a thick area. I did the same with my other foot and crowed, though softly, when I was able to lift my body toward the branch.

My hands slipped, and I toppled backward.

Turren scooped me up in his arms. "Very good effort, my treasured mate."

"Stop calling me stuff like that."

"Mate?"

"You know. Gorgeous. Lovely. Amazing. Precious. Treasured."

"But that's what you are." He tossed me up and my feet landed on the next highest branch. I grappled with the trunk to keep from falling as he joined me with one bound.

"How high are we climbing?" I'd keep trying, but I suspected my undignified way of obtaining the level he wanted for sleep wouldn't come from my own efforts but his.

"Higher. Let's try this." With that infernal grin still holding true, he linked his fingers and nudged his head, indicating I should place my foot there.

This time, when he boosted me, I was able to flop on the branch on my belly and wrangle my legs around to straddle it. I looked down at him with a victorious sneer.

He'd lost his smile, replacing it with a smoldering gaze that was locked on my exposed legs.

CHAPTER 8

TURREN

I joined my mate on the next branch and looked around, trying to ignore the sight I'd gotten of her pale legs, so slender and beautiful. Humans were peculiar creatures, small when compared to orcs, and strong, though lacking the enormous muscle mass orcs depended on.

My cock had perked up at the view, but I suppressed it as best I could. I was walking a tight wire high in the canopy and any mistake on my part could send me crashing to the ground.

"This will do," I said, placing my spear on a nearby branch and sitting with my back against the tree. My blades strapped to my waist would serve as our defense until I could grab my spear, assuming we had need. Predators rarely ventured this high in the canopy. I patted my thighs. "You'll sleep here, my luscious mate."

Words kept gushing up from my belly, and I couldn't seem to suppress them. Since I rarely spoke, I'd decided to let this new Turren guide me in regard to my mate. Would this Turren run out of words to describe her? I'd have to wait and see.

"I'll do quite fine where I am." Her finger stabbed at the branch below her feet.

I cocked one side of my brow ridge her way. "Reneging on your agreement already? I thought you'd be true to your word."

She huffed and fumed, and I gulped as her nicely rounded breasts jiggled with the movement. As if she felt the heat of my gaze there, she stilled, shooting me a glare. "Stop gaping at me."

"I was merely enjoying the view you so kindly offer."

"I'm not offering anything!"

Birds squawked and scattered from the dense vegetation around us.

My smile grew wider.

Her scowl grew deeper. "I always keep my word."

"My lips are grateful."

"Why do you want to kiss me? You don't know me. You don't care for me."

"I know that you're mine," I said with a low growl. "My fates chose you for me." I tapped my pendant lying on my chest. "I adore you already despite your snarly demeanor. You'll soon see I'm the perfect match for you."

"All that adoration and perfect match stuff aside, what do you mean when you say your fates chose you for me?"

As if she'd drawn the light to the surface with her words, my pendant blazed.

She lifted her hand to shield her eyes. "Do you have whisps trapped inside that thing?"

"This pendant was handed to me by a good friend. Every orc has a pendant like this, though the symbol is different for each clan. This symbol," I held my pendant up proudly. "Flames. They represent the clan of my heart."

"Clan of your heart?"

I . . . lost my words. Swallowing deeply, I tried to find them again. There was so much I wanted to share, yet so much I didn't dare share, not even with my mate.

I closed my eyes and found I could speak as long as I wasn't looking at her. "When an orc meets their fated mate, their perfect match, the fates bring light into their world with their pendants."

"Do you really believe such a thing is true?"

"You . . . are skeptical in addition to snarly, but in my heart, yes. I know this." Speaking softly helped as well. With my eyes open, I could still find my words. "I know that I will fall in love with you quickly, that only you will complete me, that I will cherish you until my dying day and beyond. I will be there for you when things go sour or when great joy shines in our lives."

So many words. So much spoken from the heart. Perhaps that also made the difference.

"I've told you I don't like you. There's no way I'm going to accept that I'm yours, let alone love you."

At least she said it kindly.

"I'm a patient orc." I nodded slowly. "Each day I have with you is precious. If that is only three days, then so be it."

"If . . ." She shook her head. "You seem like a decent male, but I'm not interested in having a relationship."

That was hard to accept. "Is it bad to have a male tell you he will love you beyond this life and into the next, that he will do all he can to claim your heart and your devotion?"

"It is if I don't want it," she said in a small voice. Her gaze dropped from mine, and for a heartbeat, I could tell she was seriously considering my words. But she shored up her defenses and met my gaze once more, hers full of steel. "I'll complete our bargain, and I insist that you complete yours."

I dipped my head forward. "I'm not only a patient orc, but I'm also an orc of his word. You can trust this."

She snorted. "I just met you. I don't trust anything about you."

"You trust me somewhat already. You know I will protect you, provide you with food and security, that I will ensure you reach your destination." This was a step on her part, and I was going to hold on to it tightly. "That's enough for now." I patted my lap. "Come, mate. Sit. Rest. We walk all day tomorrow."

"Let's settle a few rules first. No touching me."

"Am I to keep my arms splayed wide while you sit on my lap?"

"You know what I mean. No accidentally feeling any part of my body other than places you'd naturally need to touch."

"Not unless you ask me to."

"That will not happen." Her smile rose, making my heart pause before thumping faster. What would it be like to have her smile at me because she cared?

For one moment, fear wrapped around my chest like a thick band determined to cut off my wind. She may never love or want me. I could try my hardest, speak everything inside my heart, and she might still reject me.

But no. I cupped my pendant in my hand. The fates would not send her to me if she wasn't the one who'd make my life complete, who'd bring back the light that had been stolen from me when I was young.

"We're going to put all this aside until morning," she said. "I'm too tired to deal with it now." With that, she pivoted and plopped her ripe ass on my thighs.

My cock essentially groaned. I bit back the sound roaring up my throat.

"Will you perch on my lap all night?" I asked pleasantly. "Lean back. Allow me to wrap my arm around your waist. Then you won't fall. You'll rest easier."

"I'm fine like I am."

"Very well." While she sat with a rigid body, I tilted my head back and closed my eyes, doing my best to ignore how arousing I found the little wiggles she made while trying to get comfortable.

"You're raising your brother," I said softly. "He's much younger than you."

"Ten years. I'm not ninety or anything."

"I never suggested you were."

"I'm twenty-two, and I've raised Brunnen since he was three. Our parents died."

"You were a mother to him."

"Yes." She frowned. "I feel like I've already raised a child."

"Would you welcome your own?"

She shrugged. "I don't know. I've been a mother for ten years already."

Then I wouldn't—yet—share my secret. "I'm sorry about your parents. Mine were killed when they were caught in a landslide with my older brother. Their vox tried to save them but couldn't."

"I don't know what a vox is."

I explained.

"You raise giant birds, and they fly with you in the sky?" She sounded incredulous. She'd also relaxed against my chest. Progress.

"We're with them when they slip from the seed. They bond with us, and we raise them. We train them to take us wherever we need to travel."

She was quiet for a moment. "I'm sorry about your parents and older brother."

"Thank you." I didn't want to talk about them. Too much pain waited in that direction. "You weren't one of the two women offered in the hunt."

She shifted on my lap. "No."

"Why did you bring your brother into the woods tonight? Predators roam the forest. You're both defenseless."

"I didn't endanger him." Her voice came out shrill. "We were doing alright until you came along and made demands."

"I wasn't judging you," I said patiently. "There are many dangers here. You must have a good reason to be here at this time. This is no whim."

Her long sigh rang out. "We had to run."

"You were in danger inside the village?" A fierce need to protect her slammed through me, and I growled.

"What?" Her head darted this way and that, and she kept her voice low. "What do you see?"

"Nothing I can kill—yet."

"Are you actually upset that we felt the need to run?"

"Why sound incredulous? You're my brave mate. I will protect you until the last breath wheezes from my throat."

"That sounds dramatic to me."

I grinned. Only a human mate would see things

this way. An orc female . . . But I didn't want an orc female even if offered. I only wanted my true mate. Kaila. "Who was endangering you?"

"It doesn't matter. We fled, and we're going to the women's village. You don't need to know more than that."

"You don't need me to gut someone?"

She actually laughed. "You'd do something like that?"

"Yes."

"Why?"

"Because you're my everything."

"You shouldn't say things like that when you don't mean them."

Did she hear the croak in her voice?

"And what if I do mean them?" I asked.

"Why?" The word whined from her lungs. "It makes no sense. You just met me. You know nothing about me except my name. For all you know, I'm mean and surly, and I can't cook."

"You *are* surly."

Her low laugh rang out. "I guess I am. I've had to be strong. It's not easy raising a young boy when you're basically a child yourself, but I did it. I'm still doing it. He's amazing, and he'll be a wonderful man. I take pride in that."

"As you should." I paused, keeping my eyes closed so I could *see* my words, grab onto them, and force them past my lips. "I can cook."

"You know that's not what I'm saying."

"You're the precious woman the fates gave me."

"I'm *not* a gift."

"To me, you are. My people are dying. Fewer orclings are born each generation. Most are male. Without precious females, our clans will cease to exist."

"Are you saying you're happy I was *gifted* to you because I'm going to be a receptacle for your seed?"

"I'll happily plant my seed within you when you're ready, which you will be."

"You're much too confident of that."

"You'll see."

She huffed. "Yet you haven't even stolen the first of the kisses you demanded."

"I won't be stealing a kiss."

"You already are with your bargain."

She was right, but that wasn't my point.

"I'm not ready to kiss you yet," I said. "When I am, you'll know." I wanted her to feel it, not remain impassive to fulfill a bargain.

Her breath stilled. "I'd think you'd be all over that as soon as I sat on your lap."

"Should I kiss the back of your head?"

I realized my eyes had opened—and I could still speak. Her lips must be thinning because irritation came through in her words. "I won't enjoy your kisses. I'll grant them to you because I must, but my heart won't be in them."

"Yet."

She growled. "Are you going to talk all night, or are we going to sleep?"

"Sleep, my beautiful mate. I'll keep you safe."

I wasn't sure she'd rest, but her head started nodding backward. When she slid to the right, I placed my arm around her waist, keeping her snug against my chest.

While I didn't sleep, I dreamed.

CHAPTER 9
KAILA

"Wake, my sleepy mate."

The raspy voice tugged me from a deep sleep where I was warm, comfortable, and snuggled against . . .

"Ah!" I straightened, realizing that sometime during the night, I'd turned around and basically crawled all over Turren. My legs encircled his hips, my fingers were teasing across the warm skin on his sides, and . . . "Your cock is . . ." I gaped down at the enormous thing thrusting between us. It had dragged up his loincloth during the night and the leather barely covered it. "You're huge. How in the world do you think that will fit inside a woman of my size?"

"I assume you'll stretch?"

"You don't sound confident of that."

"Would you like to try?"

A low hum simmered in my belly, shooting down-ward. "Stretching doesn't sound pleasant."

"Because it won't be pleasant." Leaning close, he whispered by my ear. "You will enjoy it so much, you will scream."

"I'm sure screaming will be a part of anything involving that." Snatching my hands from his side, I pointed at his cock. "Put that thing down."

He slapped my rump, though not hard enough to sting. "Climb off me, mate, and I'll make my cock behave."

I scrambled off his lap. Toppling backward, I nearly fell off the branch. I would've if Turren's hand hadn't snapped out to grab onto my arm.

He tugged me back into his lap and wrapped his arms around me. "Good morning, my clumsy mate. It's a lovely day already. Hear the birds. Smell the perfume from the flowers in the air."

"Are you always this happy in the morning?"

"I'm with my fate-chosen mate. She slept sweetly in my arms last night and this morning she's eager to discuss my cock." His gaze shot to the infernal thing tenting his loincloth. "Should I give you your first kiss while the sun lifts into the sky?"

"You're awfully talkative."

"It's a wonder, isn't it?"

I had no idea what that meant.

"I don't want a kiss." I scrunched my face. "My breath tastes horrible."

"If this is about the flavor of your mouth, I don't mind."

I bet he didn't. "Release me."

"So you can fall to the ground, my beloved mate? You could be injured. While I'll happily carry you through the day as we travel, I doubt you want my arms around you that long." Laughter came through in his voice. Funny how I knew him enough already to recognize it without looking up to see the grin that must still be plastered on his face.

"Would you please take me to the ground?"

"Hey, when are we heading out?" My brother stood beneath our tree, looking up, though with all the branches and vegetation, he probably couldn't see us.

I squirmed. What would he think if he *could* see me nestling so easily in Turren's arms? Probably nothing. He was thirteen, mature in a few ways but still very innocent in others.

"Kisses can wait. Your brother waits. Our journey also awaits. If you'll untangle yourself from around me, I'll take you to the ground."

I was stroking his chest again. My bitter shriek erupted from my throat, and I flung my hands into the air. "You did this to me."

"Made you touch me, stroke me?" He kept smiling. "I believe you like me, my astonishing mate." He stood with me in his arms, holding me easily while I clung for a new reason, fear of falling down through the branches. "Never fear. Your heart is safe with me, my adorable one." He grabbed his weapon and slid it into the scabbard running down his spine.

With that, he leaped off the branch, and we soared downward.

I shrieked and closed my eyes, pressing my face into his neck, my arms and legs coiling about him like moss on a tree.

He landed squarely on the ground with barely a grunt. How he didn't break an ankle or leg was beyond me.

A trembling wreck, I whimpered and continued to cling. "You left my heart somewhere back up in the tree."

"Please, mate. Let's keep our feelings between us."

"I'm not saying I *like* you. You know what I mean."

"She likes me," Turren announced to Brunnen.

"I do not." My voice came out muffled.

Did he have to smell good? If he stunk, it would be much easier to dislike him.

"Release me, my stunning mate," he said. "I promise I'll hold you again soon."

CHAPTER 10

TURREN

I was having so much fun teasing a response out of Kaila. With words! I'd found so many, I couldn't seem to stop them from bubbling to the surface.

There was a fine line between hatred and adoration, and I intended to keep pricking her hide until the feelings blurred in her mind. Then, I would give her a kiss.

She slid down my body and stepped away, scowling.

"I rose early, climbed down the tree, and set up a few snares," Brunnen said, his feet eagerly shifting on the ground. He held up a decent sized reskit. "See?"

"Amazing," I took it from him and looked at it from all angles. "There's enough here for our breakfast. We'll have some left over to smoke and carry with us. Well done."

While he beamed, Kaila shot me a glare.

I, being the kind mate that I am, gave her a smile.

"I can see you're a good provider," I added to Burren.

His face pinkened, and he nodded. "I told Kaila I wouldn't be a burden, that we'd find a way to survive."

"Have you ever used a staff?"

His gaze shot to the one I carried in a sheath on my spine. "Not yet."

"While we walk, I'll teach you."

"You will?" he breathed, his eyes widening. "Did you hear that, Kaila? Turren's going to teach me how to fight with a staff."

"I heard him," she said sourly.

"Kaila's grumpy in the morning," Brunnen said, reaching out to ruffle her hair.

She smacked his arm and started stomping toward the woods. "I'll leave you two to continue to bond."

"I'll take your sister to the woods." I started after her.

"Great. I'll light a fire and skin and prep the meat," Brunnen said.

I caught up to Kaila and walked into the woods with her.

"I don't need you to stand guard over me," she said, stopping behind a long row of thick bushes.

"If I don't . . ." I snagged a lemist dangling from the tree above her head and tossed it into the woods. It hissed and tried to bite me, but I was able to snatch my hand away from its fangs. "You wouldn't want to step on something like that."

Her feet dancing, Kaila gasped and smacked her body. "Are there any on me? I hate lemists. Please, tell me there aren't any on me."

"Hold still." I grabbed her hands. "I promise you, my fearless mate, that I am here for you. I will watch over you. I'll protect you from all harm—including lemists." I plucked an insect out of her hair and held it between us, examining its blue spotted, black exoskeleton. Its legs scrambled and its feelers twitched.

Kaila reeled away from me. "I don't like insects either."

"And yet you planned to walk in the woods for days. You planned to sleep on the ground."

"There are bugs up in the trees. Lemists too."

"Which is why I'll hold you in my arms. How else will I keep them from getting close to you?"

She released a shiver, and her glare only grew. Truly, my mate was extra snarly this morning.

I loved it.

"Turn around," she snapped.

I did so, humming while she shifted her clothing aside and took care of her needs.

When she'd finished, she tapped my spine. "You can do your first kiss now."

I turned to face her. "I thought your breath stunk?"

Her lips scrunched together. "It's not that bad."

"I'm not ready to kiss you yet." With that, I walked deeper into the forest.

She followed quietly but only for a moment. "Where are we going? You're not taking me back to my brother."

"I'm looking for wood to make his staff. It needs to be large enough so he'll still be able to use it for a few years as he grows. Yet not too unwieldy to learn with now."

"You don't have to be nice to him to impress me."

"Is that what you think I'm doing? Perhaps I like him. Perhaps I want to teach him a skill you can't. Perhaps I want to do this for him."

She paused, and I stopped with her. "I'm sorry."

"For what in particular, my charming mate?"

"For making assumptions. You said something about wooing me, and I assumed this was part of the process."

"I see." Spying a downed limb, long and slender and straight and without any rot, I made my way over to it and hefted it. "When I woo you, you'll know it. When I kiss you, you'll want it. And when we fully mated, you'll crave it."

She huffed. "Just when we start to have a normal conversation, you bring all that junk into it."

"You don't want a mate you crave?"

"If I ever choose to mate, it'll be for practical reasons."

I started stripping the bark off the branch with my blade. "Such as?"

"Someone who'll be a good protector and provider. Someone who won't make too many demands. He'll stand beside me and support me but stay out of my way."

I chuckled about the last. "In all this, you already have your perfect mate—me."

"I don't want you for a mate."

"As you say . . . now." Once the bark had been removed, I sliced off the thin, smaller twigs branching off the staff. "You'll change your mind."

I lobbed off the ends of the branch and held it up, nodding. This would do nicely.

"Within three days? You're dreaming, Turren. Dreaming." She started stomping to our right.

I looped my arm around her waist, lifted her off the ground, and planted her on the forest floor facing in the right direction. "This way, my delectable mate." I gave her a nudge to get her started.

"I knew that was the right way," she huffed. "I was just . . . enjoying the view in the other direction."

"Yes. I see." Following her, I grinned. My mate was a pure delight.

She didn't even realize I was wooing her already.

CHAPTER II
KAILA

Turren cut a plant we used to clean our teeth, pointing it out to us both so we could find it for ourselves. While we brushed at the river, he dug tubers and picked berries. We ate a hearty meal, washing it down with water. We filled flasks for us to carry. Then we started walking.

Brunnen swung his new staff around, hitting trees and swiping it through bushes.

"You'll need to smooth the grip," Turren said, walking beside my brother.

"What do you mean?" Brunnen asked.

Turren showed him. He was kind and patient with my brother, something few other than me had bothered to do. Most saw him as either a barrier in getting to me, like my boss, or a pain for asking so many questions.

Turren listened and showed Brunnen which rocks

would work best not only for smoothing the handle of his new staff but sharpening the tip.

"After we stop tonight, and before it gets dark," he said, "I'll show you some basic defensive moves. I want you to practice them for at least an hour and know right now that you'll be sore in the morning. But with more practice, they'll become seamless. They might seem silly at first, but when you can do them almost in your sleep, you'll find they come natural in battle. They could save your life."

Brunnen nodded and worked on the grip while he walked, smoothing it with the rock, while Turren pointed out plants that were edible and those we needed to avoid.

At one point, he plucked a flower and presented it to me.

"Wooing?" I asked, looking at it without touching it, though I was tempted. It was hard to maintain a surly attitude with someone who treated you kindly. If only treating him nicely didn't mean I wanted to mate with him, a common attitude with most men I'd interacted with. Smile and they thought you wanted to have sex.

"When I woo, you'll know," Turren said.

Brunnen snorted. "Kaila might not be able to tell."

Turren flashed his tusks my way, and I didn't like it. It made that hum in my belly drop lower. I was aware of him, of his pleasant scent, the way his muscles played beneath his golden green skin as he moved, and the way my skin tingled when he looked at me.

I also didn't like his flower. It was pretty but everything gifted to me in the past came with conditions. One flower might mean I had to be nice to him whether I wanted to or not.

When I didn't take it, he gently tucked the stem behind my ear, adjusting the blossom to sit at my temple. Then the floral scent kept reminding me that he'd given it to me.

Another thing I didn't like.

We stopped to eat the smoked meat for lunch and then continued walking.

By late afternoon, I was sweaty, irritable, and tired of guarding myself to avoid noticing all the wonderful things about Turren. It wasn't just his physical appearance that attracted me or the kindness he extended to my brother. With each gesture, he showed me caring, from holding back a branch on the path so it didn't scrape me to lifting me over a fallen log and gently setting me on the other side. When we stopped for lunch, he not only filled our flasks at the river, but he also wet a scrap of cloth for me and nodded while I used it to wipe off my face.

He was too nice. Too appealing. And too virile for my taste. Oh, I'd like to taste him alright. A strange melty sensation kept sliding through my bones whenever the thought flitted through my mind.

I had to keep reminding myself I had to tell him goodbye in two days.

Why hadn't he wanted to kiss me last night or this morning? I'd gotten to the point where I couldn't stop looking at his mouth. Would his tusks press into my cheeks in an unpleasant way, or would I even notice they were there? His lips were a darker green than his skin, and slightly plumper on the bottom than the top. What would they feel like moving on mine? And his tongue . . . Well, I didn't like thinking about his tongue —or that I was intrigued about it as well.

To kiss me, he'd have to lift me or scrunch over, because he was much too tall for me to reach.

If only I could stop thinking about Turren in general.

Would it feel unpleasant, or would I enjoy it? Would the itch burning inside me go away after one kiss?

When the sun was hugging the horizon, we stopped near a bend in the river.

Turren waded into the water and soon caught a fish. Another. He kept tossing them up onto the shore while Brunnen laughed and grabbed them. In no time, the two males had gutted and cleaned them. I, feeling useless, collected wood for a fire.

I was laying wood on the level area above the river when something plopped onto the ground beside me. I frowned at it before realizing what it was—Turren's wet loincloth.

Lifting my head, I gaped when I found Turren swimming in the river. "Where's . . . my brother?" He was nowhere around.

"He's bathing not far upstream, within shouting distance."

"Bathing."

"We're hot. Sweaty. We want to be clean." The heat of his gaze traveled down my frame. "You're welcome to bathe with me."

I crossed my arms over my chest. "Maybe I don't want to bathe with you." I did. Well, not necessarily bathe with him, but bathe in general. I was also hot and sweaty, plus dirty from lugging wood.

"Take off your clothing," he rasped. "Enter the water."

"Why are you so determined about this?"

"You could persuade me to give you our first kiss."

"At this rate, with you holding your kisses back, I'm beginning to think you're averse to kissing *me*."

"Never doubt that I want to kiss you, touch you, stroke you," he said softly.

I gingerly stepped down the bank to the edge of the water. "You shouldn't say such things."

"It feels good to be clean. Refreshing. Are you sure I can't talk you into coming into the water with me?"

"Talk, talk, talk. That's all you ever do."

His head tilted and then he smiled. "I am talking a lot. I like it. You should get used to it."

"I'd rather not." With a huff, I started stomping

downstream. "I'll bathe someplace else." I froze when he spoke.

"Alone?"

I whirled to face him, finding him standing with water gliding down his muscular chest. It wasn't fair that he was so attractive. If only he was old and wrinkly and boring. Anyone but *him*.

"I've bathed alone all my life," I said.

"In the forest with dusk falling?"

A creature cried out in the forest, and my body was suddenly wracked with the chills. "I won't bathe."

"You'll sleep better if you do, but I'm not one to force anyone to do something they don't wish to."

"Except kisses."

"Have I forced a kiss on you yet?"

"No, but you keep teasing me about them, making me . . ."

"Making you what, my precious mate?"

"Stop using words like that."

"You mean stating you're beautiful, treasured, and beyond compare? I only speak the truth."

And his words kept thrilling through me. "I'm none of those things."

"To me, you are, and so much more."

There was such simple honesty in his voice. And longing. It touched me in a place where no one else had ventured before, where no one had ever *cared* to venture before.

"Turn around," I croaked.

He did so without question.

I quickly removed my skirt and blouse but remained in my underwear. I wasn't that foolish. This male would never take advantage of me. I already knew this in my bones. But if I held out my hand, he'd not only take it, but he'd also tug me into his arms and . . .

He'd make me crave him.

Once I was submerged, I closed my eyes and floated, savoring how wonderful the cool water felt.

I drifted closer to Turren, joining him, I supposed, because I didn't make the effort to shift in a different direction.

"I'll wash your hair if you want." He held up the soap.

"Thank you."

He moved closer and braced me against his front with his legs around my thighs, holding me in place.

I couldn't help it. As he worked the soap into my hair and massaged my scalp, I closed my eyes and relaxed. I *enjoyed* his touch.

He carefully rinsed my hair, keeping the soap out of my eyes, then handed the bar to me. I washed my body while he studied the vegetation along the shore, looking up and downstream, keeping his gaze focused on anything and everything but me.

"What happened to your parents?" he asked softly.

"They died ten years ago."

"When you were twelve, just a girl."

"Just a girl," I agreed.

"I'm sorry. I lost my parents as well, but I was older."

"How old are you now?" I asked.

"Thirty."

"Very old."

His low laugh rang out. "Too old?"

"No. Not too old."

"That's a relief, my inquisitive mate."

My snort echoed around us. "Inquisitive?"

"I'm hoping you'll ask me more questions because I want to share. But first, tell me what it was like raising your brother. My brother and I weren't close, and I was the youngest. The . . ."

"The what?"

"I . . . My family wasn't . . . friendly."

He sounded so lonely; I wanted to hug him. And I sensed there was a lot more to his statement than I was hearing. Hoping it would make him feel more comfortable speaking, I floated beside him, doing my share of studying the forest.

"It was a very sad time in my life," he said simply. "It's hard to . . . lose family."

"I had my brother." Many times, I'd resented him. I hadn't wanted to be a parent. I had dreams of studying with the baker, of learning to craft delicious breads and pastries. "I mourned my parents, but I couldn't release all the pain inside me. My brother was devastated. He kept asking me where they were, when they'd be back, and no matter how many times I told him what happened, even when keeping my explanation simple, he'd wake up the next morning and ask me all over again."

"You trapped all your feelings inside."

"If I hadn't, my emotions would've scared him. He needed me to be there for him because they no longer were."

"Who was there for Kaila?'

"No one. We had no living family. We didn't even own our home. It belonged to the man running the gardens. If I hadn't started working for him, we would've had to move out."

"You were just a child yourself."

How could this male understand when everyone in the village had shrugged and told me to take care of what needed to be done? "No one offered to take us in or even to cook us a meal." My throat was so tight with pain, I could barely breathe.

"I'm sorry."

"Did everyone tell you to just get on with it in your village?"

"My village . . . No."

I waited, but he didn't say anything further. "Now you're a clan caedos. Did you want to be the leader?"

"At first? No. But I was persuaded." His low laugh rang out.

I nodded. "You also took on a mantle you weren't prepared to assume."

"I had a choice. No one is forced to be caedos. It wasn't a role I was raised for. I wanted to be me, whoever that was, not the leader everyone needed."

"You found a way to do it."

"It wasn't long before I was happy I'd been asked."

His kindness and caring would make him an excellent leader.

"How did you and your brother survive?" he asked.

"I cooked, cleaned our home, and went to work in the gardens. If I didn't work, we didn't eat. My parents didn't leave behind much money."

"I imagine there were times when you felt as lost as your brother."

All the time. "Just once, I wanted someone kind to lean on. Someone to listen and care when I spoke, to tell me I was doing well with Brunnen when I worried all the time that I didn't have what it took to be a mother to a small boy."

"You did well. He's a strong, responsible youngling."

I shrugged. "I did the best I could, and I suppose that was enough."

"Why leave the village now? It's been ten years. You've thrived."

Just barely. "My boss told me if I didn't go to his bed, he'd fire me."

He growled, his hand tightening on mine. When had our fingers linked together?

"Once I've left you at the women's village," he snarled, "I'll return to yours and kill him."

"Kill him for looking for a bedmate?"

"For trying to force you to do something you didn't want to."

"Yes, I didn't want to be with him that way, but I did need the job. So, we ran. We packed our things and fled in the night. Perhaps we were unwise to pick the night of the hunt, but we thought it would provide a distraction. Everyone was focused on the two women being sent out the front gate. I doubted anyone noticed we'd left through the back."

"Tell me his name, and I'll bring you his head. I mean this. I *promise* you this. With everything inside me, I will see it done."

He sounded determined. I wanted to laugh or sigh. There was something oddly endearing about a male who was desperate to defend my honor.

"Don't bother. He means nothing, and he's not worth you risking your life to kill him. We left. We're traveling to a new home." A new home without Turren.

Why did that thought make me feel sad?

CHAPTER 12

TURREN

My mate was beautiful on the inside where it counted.

She was rip-my-heart-from-my-chest-and-hand-it-to-her gorgeous. The longing inside me only grew the more I got to know her. She'd shared with me tonight, and I'd cherish that forever. It was wonderful to talk with her without her snapping or distrusting me.

I would build on that because there was no other mate for me but this one.

I understood why she resisted me. If she was like most humans, she'd only heard horrible things about orcs. To her, I was basically a beast, a male who'd rut with her without her consent, who'd claim her and take her far from everything she loved.

Again, I reminded myself to be patient. I still had

two days to show her I wasn't someone to fear, that I was someone she could love.

I wanted to watch her leave the water, but I also wanted her to see she could trust me. I turned away while she strode up onto the bank, dried, and dressed in clean clothing.

She, in turn, studiously washed her clothing, avoiding looking my way as I did the same.

After I was dressed, I helped her hang her clothing on tree limbs, and we started a fire. I could hear her brother approaching along the shore, and while I enjoyed talking with Brunnen, I would miss this time alone with Kaila.

"I have something for you." I said quickly, holding out my clasped hand. "It's a simple thing, but I saw it and thought of you."

She frowned.

I tried not to flounder, to remember that with her, I could find my words. "Usually," I swallowed hard, "these aren't found around here."

"What aren't found around here?"

"They're beneath the ground."

"I see."

She didn't. Panic rushed through me. I was messing this up, and I didn't know how to fix it. "It was sparkling. In the water. I . . . thought of you."

Her head tilted, and her gaze shot to mine. I sensed a touch of vulnerability there, and I ached to smooth any fear from her soul.

Please, mate. Know that you can believe in me. In us.

"What is it?" she asked, her voice guarded.

I stilled my floundering heart and made my tongue work as I opened my fingers, revealing the green stone lying on my palm. "It's an emerst stone. They're rare." Giving this to her meant something to me, and I hoped she'd one day see that, that she'd one day feel the way I did for her. "When you're angry—"

"Snarly, you mean," she said with a touch of humor, her fingers hovering over the smooth, flat stone but not touching. "Snarly is actually quite a good way to describe me, wouldn't you say?"

"Oh, no no. No. No." *Stop saying no.* "Never."

She was the mate I'd hoped to be with, the one I could talk to, touch, and share everything locked within me. I had a lot to give. So much, I felt like my heart would explode at times, that it surely couldn't hold this much emotion inside without the feelings clawing their way free.

She lifted the stone and held it up in the waning daylight. "It's beautiful."

"It reminds me of your eyes when you're . . . snarly."

Her lips curved up in the prettiest smile. My soul ached to see that expression on her face every day for the rest of my life.

"Do my eyes really look like this?" When she turned it, it sparkled, shooting green bands toward the forest floor.

"Yes. I can string it on leather if you'd like. Like a necklace. That you'd wear. It would look . . . nice on you." Would she reject my offer? Wearing a gift from me might feel too intimate.

"Thank you. I'd like that."

My shoulders loosened, and the bursting feeling in my heart slipped away. I wasn't a male who talked much about feelings, but with Kaila, I wanted to share everything if I could only figure out how. I worried telling her too much would make her back away.

"I'll make a hole on one edge," I said. "I won't break it."

"I know you won't."

"I'll present it to you when it's ready." She gave it back to me, and I carefully tucked it into the small pouch on the inside of my loincloth waistband. I sometimes kept coins there or bits of my world that caught my eye.

She laid her hand on my arm and started to speak, but Brunnen appeared from the trail winding along the riverbank and strode over to us.

He hefted his spear. "I practiced after bathing, Turren. Want to see?"

"Yes." My voice came out gruff. What would she have said if her brother hadn't arrived? I wanted to know. *Needed* to know.

After lighting the fire, I collected my whisp lamp from my bag and walked over to the open area adjacent to where we'd made camp. With the lamp generating just enough light to see, I stood to the side, watching as Brunnen carefully went through the moves I'd taught him.

"You're doing well," I said when he finished.

His smile practically lit up the area, and it reminded me so much of Kaila that the bursting feeling started to grow again within my heart. Could I take this overwhelming, wonderful feeling or would it tear me apart?

We cooked our meal and ate well.

"More?" I offered Kaila, who'd chosen to sit beside me with Brunnen on her other side.

"Oh, no thank you. I couldn't eat anything else."

When Brunnen shook his head, I carefully placed what was left in coated fabric and tucked it into my bag. We'd eat it in the morning. I also removed a few tools and stuffed them into my loincloth waistband.

With my whisp lantern guiding our way, we went to the river for a drink and to cleanse our mouths and teeth. After, Kaila followed Brunnen and I as we walked through the adjacent forest to select a tree.

"What about this one?" he asked, pointing. "It's tall, and I see branches high up where I can rest."

I held my lamp close to the trunk. "See this." I pointed to where insects had burrowed beneath the bark. They studiously climbed both up the trunk and toward the ground, many carrying bits of crushed vegetation. "They're nesting in this one and they'll find you."

Brunnen squinted upward, though it wasn't easy to see even with the lamp. "Way up there?"

"Would you like to chance it? These insects bite."

He shook his head.

We walked farther and when he chose another tree, I nodded with a smile of approval. "Yes. This one."

"Watch." He jumped up and grabbed onto the lowest branch. He hitched his heels on the limb and shifted his body to lie on the top. Standing, he grinned down at us. "Look, Kaila. If I ever have to travel through the forest on my own, I'll be able to pick a tree and climb it."

"You're leaning quickly, youngling," I said with pride.

He beamed and leaped again, latching onto the branch above, climbing farther.

"Would you like to select our tree, my contented mate?" I asked. Funny how I could speak when I focused on describing her current mood.

"Sure." She started walking, crooking her neck to look at the trees. "Do you believe I'm content?"

"I hope you are."

"My belly's full. My brother's happy. I'm . . ." She swallowed. "I *am* content. You named me true this evening."

Progress. It was all I could do not to shout out my joy. *I* was much more than content.

I'd found hope.

"What about this one?" She stopped beside a tree, leaning close to it. "I don't see any insects, and the limbs above appear wide and smooth."

Looking up, I grunted. "A good choice. Do you need anything before we ascend?"

She shook her head.

"Will you let me carry you?" I asked.

"Alright." Her eyes darted up to my face, and I wished I knew what her expression meant. Fear? No, not that. Nervousness? Not that either. Ah, yes, I knew.

She was *still* content.

I wasn't sure I could bear the aching feeling in my chest.

I lifted her gently and, holding her in one arm, leaped onto the first branch above.

"Orcs are nothing like human men," she said softly.

I jumped to the next branch and studied the ones above, selecting the next. "In what way?"

"Men can be . . . surly."

"You must feel comfortable with that attitude." I said in all seriousness.

She frowned before her light laughter trilled out. I'd heard her laugh with her brother while walking today, but with me, she'd only been serious.

And surly.

"Funny." She smacked my chest, though not hard. More like a tap that showed affection.

My pulse surged, having nothing to do with my

exertions. If only I could hear her laugh with me like this all the time.

"We have a definite class system in the village," she said. "And I don't only mean those who have and those who don't. My brother and I were in the group without. We struggled to survive. But there's also a class system among the sexes. Women there are considered . . . inferior."

"Truly?"

"You sound amazed."

"I am."

"It must be the same with orcs."

"Not at all. Females and males are different. While some female orcs are as strong as any of our males, many are not."

"See? Orcs give more value to strength, which is only one small part of a person."

"I didn't say that." I tried to collect my thoughts while studying the branches above. "Some females are as strong as males. Females in my clan—no, in *all* orc clans as far as I know—are not valued solely on the might of their arms." I jumped again, landing squarely on a higher branch. Two more and we could settle for the night. Another leap, and I planted my boots on the next.

"I suppose it's the same everywhere," she said sadly. "A woman can tell the world she wants to control her own life, but all it takes is one man, a man who might not even be family, to state he will claim her, and everyone agrees."

"Ah. You saw me claiming you as me announcing that I would take control of your future."

"I won't let anyone do that to me. I ran from the village because a man was making demands. I could've complained to the mayor, but he's not a good person. I doubt he would care. He probably would've told me to climb into my boss's bed and be glad someone wanted me."

"I claimed you as all orcs have for as long back as any orc can remember."

"It feels like the same thing to me."

I landed on the branch I'd selected and settled with my back to the trunk, my legs stretched out in front of me. This tree was so large, it towered over many of its friends. I could shift on the branch while we slept without fear of falling.

Kaila sat on my lap, facing sideways. Better than facing away where I couldn't see her expression.

"All are respected in my clan," I said. "I mean this. Not only for what they can offer others, but for who they are at their very core." I tapped my chest. "If this was not true, I would not be caedos."

"I don't see the connection."

"Then you haven't noticed my arm."

"I did. I was going to ask about it but decided you'd tell me what happened if and when you wanted to."

"You see that this arm isn't as strong as the other."

"I didn't notice any difference when you climbed the tree while holding me."

"There is. I have fought for much of my life to prove to everyone . . ." Hating that I was nearly shouting, I lowered my voice. "I have proven I am worthy." I tapped the trunk behind me. "Do you think one tree has more value than another?"

She shrugged. "I guess if one's bigger, it has more value for the wood it can provide."

"One could say it overpowers the others, much like you describe the men in your village. A tree this large has an enormous canopy. Its leaves stretch highest to the sun and thus, it shades those below who then gain less nutrients from the light. But it also provides shelter from storms, blocking much of the wind. It doesn't see the smaller trees as competition. It doesn't feel that their slighter bodies have less value."

"I doubt trees think of anything like that."

"You don't believe trees think of anything other than stretching toward the light and sucking up water with their roots?"

"They're not sentient."

"Some of these trees are."

Her gaze darted around. "You mean they're watching, listening?"

"Nothing like that." I lifted my pendant, which blazed with light once more. "Wanderers are special people within the clans. They travel, testing tones with their pendants to discover everything the world around us has to offer."

Her head tilted. "It's just a piece of metal, isn't it?"

"Watch." I gently blew across my pendant, creating a low tone that rumbled across my skin.

The light went out.

Her breath caught, but she huffed. "You can't prove that you made your pendant stop flaring by creating that sound."

"That wasn't why I blew across it."

"Then why?"

I untied my whisp lantern from my waistband and held it up, puffing air across the small creature nestled inside. The insects flitted about, and we collected them, giving them a home in a clear round plant. There, they laid eggs that hatched to replace the parent.

The whisp emitted a low glow.

"More blowing." She sounded disappointed. "You're not doing anything I couldn't do. This doesn't prove trees are sentient."

"No?" Turning, I hung my lantern on the thin branch curving down from the canopy above. It rocked, making the glow float around us.

"I don't see what you mean," she said a bit sadly.

I took the lantern back and blew across my pendant.

The thin branch coiled back up among the others above.

"Hold on," Kaila said in awe. "Did . . .?"

I nodded, grinning. "Watch." Another puff of air across my pendant, and the branch descended once more. I hung the lantern on it, and with another tone from my pendant, asked the tree if it would please hold our light through the night. The leaves above trembled, giving me the answer.

"You . . . I don't know what to say. I've heard of magic, but it's just something out of stories, isn't it?"

"It's not magic unless you consider the wanderers as orcs who can create it magical as well. I spoke to the tree with the tone, proving it not only heard but it responded. Sentient, in a slight way."

"I'm . . . amazed. Stunned." She sighed. "I can see what you mean about the relationships of trees, but that doesn't apply to humans. Women are not considered equal in my village, and I suspect that will never change."

"Not until minds are changed first."

"How does someone do a thing like that?"

"It takes more than one person, and it takes persistence, proving one's worth many times until it sinks in so deeply, they can't see you in any other way."

"You're speaking of your arm now."

My throat tight, I could only nod. Did she see me as defective? My parents had.

"I'm sorry. I imagine it was very painful." Her gaze remained on the limb. "When it happened."

"Horribly."

"I'm sorry. When you want to talk about it, I'm ready to listen."

"One day, perhaps."

"Like one day, women might be considered equal to men. I'm one such being with very little power. Some women have started to say no. They left their village and built a new one. We're traveling there. I've only dreamed of having complete say in my own life, and I'm excited to think that there, finally, I'll be considered equal to all the others."

She was still determined to tell me goodbye. So much strength in such a tiny person. I admired her greatly. But it was going to hurt when she walked away.

"You'll find life in the new village much different from the one you left behind." I didn't want to leave her there. I still had one more day of travel and two nights before we'd reach the village.

Was that enough time to convince her we were meant to be together?

"You mentioned my claiming you," I said. "For orcs, claiming a mate is a mutual thing."

"You may have noted that I didn't agree, so it wasn't mutual for us." She moved to face me, her legs going around my waist.

Did she realize she was calmly accepting this position, that we'd sleep with our arms around each other as if we truly were the mates I'd proclaimed?

"I did note that," I said gruffly. "When orcs are

chosen by the fates, they both are excited. One claims the other and the words are repeated, thus making it a mutual thing."

"Just like that, a couple is happy to let the fates play such a large role in their future?"

"For us, it's sacred, something we long for our entire lives. It's rare for the fates to pair a couple."

"What if one of them loves another?"

I lifted her chin to meet her eyes. "Do you love another?"

"I've never been in love."

A relief. How could I compete with a shadow? "Do you long to love someone?"

"Not if it means giving up my soul."

I treasured how strong willed and independent she was. If only I could show her that I wanted a mate who'd stand beside me, not in my shadow. "When two love," I closed my eyes to help find the words. If I could see them in my mind, I could say them, "They're not giving anything up. They want to share all they are with the other."

"I can't imagine a love like that." Her words came out wistfully, and when I opened my eyes, she wrenched her gaze from mine, planting it on my chest.

"What if a love like that was given to you?"

"By the fates?"

I nodded, grateful she was discussing this with me and not arguing.

"I'm not sure I could believe it was true."

"And if it was?"

"I believe I'd grab onto such a love and cling tight. Nothing and no one would tear us apart."

"And that, my pensive mate, is what I hope we'll find together."

"We only have two more nights and one day together." Her gaze dropped to my mouth. "And you still haven't kissed me."

"Maybe I'm waiting for *you* to kiss *me*."

Her tongue, so tiny and pink, dipped out to stroke across her lips.

I bit back my groan. My cock ignored my will and started to stiffen.

"We should sleep," she finally said, looking to the right. "Can you turn down the lantern?'

I blew the request across my pendant, and the branch lifted enough that we still had light, but it was muted.

"Goodnight, Turren," she said softly. "I . . . You're not like anyone I've ever met before. I . . . like you."

My pulse thudded louder than the drums we beat during celebrations.

"Goodnight, Kaila. You're unlike any other. I like you too."

Her lips curled up on one side.

Before I could blink, she rose up onto her knees and placed her mouth on mine. Just as quickly, she backed away, though her fingers remained tight on my arms.

"First kiss," she said, her voice breathy.

"That was a quick kiss."

"You didn't specify how long they needed to be."

I teased my fingertips up and down her sides. She didn't pull away. Her eyelids fluttered, and a shiver skipped through her. Looking up at me, humor shone in her eyes. "I guess you'd better make sure the second one lasts longer then."

I sucked in a breath, not daring to believe she'd said such a thing. It was all I could do to make my tongue work to give her a reply. "I believe I should."

"Until tomorrow, then."

"Only one full day left." Despair clogged my throat. A lot could happen in one day. "I'll have to find a way to fit in two long kisses."

"I . . ." A touch of longing came through in her words. "I look forward to it." Her husky laughter rang out, smoothing across my skin and plunging down into my cock. The foolish thing responded as if it thought one simple kiss could lead to so much more.

In no time, her breathing leveled off. She mumbled something and snuggled deeper in my arms. In her sleep, she sought me.

I'd cling to the idea that this meant something and pray to the fates that tomorrow I could make a difference.

I wasn't being completely honest with her about my life with my clan, but how could I share everything? I'd wait and tell her when the time was right. And I hoped that time would be soon.

While she rested, I carefully took out the tools I'd removed from my bag.

Then with the whisp lantern guiding me, I quietly began working on the stone.

CHAPTER 13

KAILA

I wasn't lying when I told Turren I liked him. It was hard not to like him. He wasn't like any man I'd meant before. He didn't make demands, and he made me laugh. I'd barely have to think about something I needed before he'd spontaneously hand it to me. A seed cake while we walked. Cool water from the river. He even knew when to suggest we stop and rest.

We had breakfast the next morning and started walking.

"You need to rest," he said mid-morning, nudging his chin toward a downed branch. "Sit, please."

Brunnen slipped into the woods while I dropped to the branch with a heavy sigh.

"I'm not used to walking," I said. "Back in the village, I worked in the town's gardens, weeding and planting, then harvesting in the fall. I worked hard, and I'm tough, but it's not the same thing."

"I'm sure your feet are sore." He dropped to his knees in front of me. Seeing him like this made my heart flutter.

If I wasn't careful, I'd more than like this male.

I smiled. "All of me is sore. Who knew this many muscles would be taxed by walking?"

"It's all right to take breaks." He sucked in a breath and released it. "It's finished." He carefully pulled the stone strung on a strip of leather from his tiny pouch. When he lifted it, it caught the sun, fracturing it into green beams around us.

"It's gorgeous," I breathed, meeting his gaze. I was honored. I'd cherish this forever. "Thank you. It's pretty. Knowing . . . well, knowing that you made it for me means a lot."

"Would you like me to secure it around your neck?"

"Yes, please." I leaned closer, closing my eyes because he smelled yummy. Like a foreign spice, plus all male. He tied the strip of leather around my neck and smoothed my hair, his fingers lingering.

Back in the village, if someone told me I would one day not only like an orc, but that an odd longing would fill me whenever he was near, I would've scoffed and told them they were out of their mind. But the more I got to know Turren, the more I started fearing our arrival at the village because that meant I'd have to tell him goodbye. He was the leader of a clan far from the place I'd chosen for our new home. There was no way we could spend more time together.

And what would I hope to achieve by being near him longer? I didn't know, but I could barely resist the urge to cling.

Because the thought scared me, I leaned back when he was finished, staring down at the pendant. Lifting it to admire it in the light. "Thank you."

He stroked my face, his fingers light enough I could either pull away or lean into his touch. Everything inside me wanted to close my eyes again and just *feel* . . .

When Brunnen walked back into the clearing, I was both miffed at him for interrupting and thankful, because I suspected if he hadn't arrived, I would've given Turren his second kiss, and I would've made sure it lasted a lot longer.

My brother sat on the end of the log and ate.

Turren removed my shoes and socks.

I stared down at him. "What are you doing?"

He shot me a smile that made my core throb. He pulled a small container from the pouch he wore secured to his lower back and opened it. A pungent, minty aroma drifted through the air. After scooping some of the creamy substance out, he sat and placed my foot on his lap.

He started massaging the cream into my foot.

At first it tickled. Then it felt amazing. Releasing

guttural laughter, I squirmed on the log. My laughter turned to moans.

Turren kept shooting me smiles that weren't only given but accepted. I couldn't help but smile back.

He finished with one foot and dressed it again, gently placing it inside my shoe and securing the fastenings. Lifting my other foot, he gave it equal attention.

By then, I'd started to wonder what his magical fingers would feel like on my breasts. My thighs. The place between them. The burn low in my belly shot downward. It was all I could do not to lift my skirt, lean back, and tell Turren in no uncertain terms that he needed to take care of the second fire he'd sparked.

Where had this Kaila come from?

I suspected Turren had brought her to the surface.

Gathering more of the cream, he spread it up my leg in broad circles. The muscles twitched. The simmer in my bones ignited. I couldn't stop moaning. Turren's smiles had grown more seductive. He knew exactly what he was doing to me.

"You two are weird." Brunnen grabbed my flask from the log beside me and removed Turren's from his pouch. "I'll go fill these." With a boyish huff, he stalked toward the river that was close enough, I could see it from where I sat. He stomped down the bank to the water, disappearing from view.

Turren took more cream and continued stroking

my legs, his hands moving higher. Soon, he was massaging my thighs.

I spread them wider and leaned back against a tree. I couldn't help it. I was so far gone, he could do whatever he pleased, and I wouldn't stop him.

"My brother," I gasped out, struggling to stop myself from sinking so deeply into his touch I wouldn't be aware of anything going on around me. My brother could return any minute . . .

"Orcs have amazing hearing." His fingers stilled. "Unless you'd like me to stop."

"No," I moaned.

His fingers teased higher. I spread my legs wider.

"You smell delicious," he growled. "I want to taste you."

How decadent. What would it be like to slip off my undergarment, to lay on the ground and let him do it? I was gasping at the thought already. Slick with need already.

"Whatever my sensual mate needs, I'm going to deliver," he rasped. With each rub, his finger bumped my clit, each nudge shooting me higher into the sky. I'd only been with a few men, and each time, I'd left their beds feeling unsatisfied. I suspected I'd not only be satisfied in Turren's bed, but that I might never want to leave it.

"Don't stop," I moaned.

One of his hands continued to stroke. Leaning over me, shielding me with his enormous body, he kept rubbing my legs, working out the kinks in each muscle. His other hand slid my undergarment to the side and dipped beneath. A finger teased through my wetness.

He growled. "Fuck. Mate . . ."

Bracing my legs apart with his hand, he continued to glide his fingers through my wetness, dipping into my entrance before pulling out and coasting across my clit.

Overcome with sensations I'd never found with another, I bucked beneath him. I was too far gone. Nothing was going to bring me back to the present.

He drove a few fingers inside me and lifted my skirt, burying his face between my legs. A long lick through my wetness was followed by him sucking my clit into his mouth.

I groaned and shifted my hips, grinding my body against his mouth.

His head jerked up, and he shot a glance over his shoulder before dragging his fingers from my saturated passage. He slid my undergarment back into place and tugged down my skirt, leaning back on his heels.

Brunnen stomped back into the clearing with the full flasks, nonchalantly dropping two of them on the ground beside Turren before taking his staff and striding to the middle of the open area. His back to us, he went through the moves Turren had taught him.

My eyes fell on Turren again, fusing with his. While I watched, mesmerized, he licked his lips.

Then he sucked and licked his fingers clean of my wetness.

I couldn't look away. The hum building inside my body was a furious beast making demands, telling me in no uncertain terms that it wanted this male more than any other and *now*.

I was in trouble. Big trouble.

Because I couldn't wait until tonight to find out if he'd put out the fire he'd started.

As we walked throughout the afternoon, all I could think about was the pleasure Kaila had found from my touch.

The heady flavor of her flesh. The way her body had taken my fingers so sweetly. And the way she'd moaned and thrust her hips up to meet my thrusts with complete abandon.

She hadn't surrendered to me, and I wasn't sure I'd want someone who would, but she was softening. My patience and persistence were paying off.

Tonight, I'd claim a kiss and see what happened after that.

"Would you like to hear about my desert home?" I asked Kaila. She'd been striding in the middle of us along a narrow shayde trail with her brother taking the lead, but the trail had widened, and she'd dropped back to walk beside me.

Brunnen remained ahead of us, slashing at thick branches with his staff, perfecting the thrusts I'd taught him once I could drag my mind away from my pretty mate's luscious body and focus on the situation at hand.

I needed to be alert for threats, not consumed by my need to continue pleasuring my mate.

"Tell me," she said.

"First, we're a migratory clan, though we spend about half our year near the vox breeding grounds."

"I've heard of voxes," Brunnen said over his shoulder. With a grunt, he thrust his spear forward as if to impale an attacking predator, following the gouge with a kick high enough to hit a head with the intent to stun, another trick I'd taught him.

"You have?" Kaila sent me a bemused look. Whenever I caught her gaze, color flooded her face, and she dragged her eyes away. But when she appeared to think I wasn't looking, her attention would lock again on me. I wasn't sure what she was thinking, but I'd ask as soon as we were alone.

I had to know if she was beginning to more than like me. I hated to think her response was only her body speaking and not her heart and mind.

"Yes, they're huge birds and the orcs ride on their backs," Brunnen said.

"The Ember Clan is the keeper of the voxes. They leave with their newly bonded orcs, but every few years, they return to breed. They're not the best parents, which is why we're there to help. While the parents leave to return to their orcs, we remain by the seeds. Orcs travel from other clans to bond with a vox youngling the moment it slips from its seed. We show them how to train the vox as it matures, and when they're ready, they take to the skies and return to their own clan."

"I want to ride a vox," Brunnen said in awe. "It must be amazing. You're high up and powerful."

"It's wonderful." If Kaila chose to go with me back to my desert home, Brunnen would come with us. He could bond with a vox. I was sure humans could do so. Why not? I'd be with him, cheering for him as he explored the wonder of his first vox. "Just like on the ground, however, there are dangers in the sky. But with training, a warrior and his or her vox will be prepared to meet them."

"Like me." Brunnen slashed his spear through a thin branch blocking the path.

"Like you," I agreed with a smile I shared with Kaila. "Would you like to bond with a vox?"

"Humans can bond with them?" Her voice came out in jerky gasps. "I'm not sure I'd want something like that."

"Why not?"

"Isn't it scary?"

"It's unlike anything else in the world. You're one with the creature, soaring through the air and diving to the ground."

"They're like a pet?"

"In some ways."

"Does flying around like that upset your belly?"

"You get used to it. You don't start out with complex maneuvers. The orc and the vox are taught at a pace they can build on."

Biting her lower lip, she nodded. "Maybe it would be nice. To try."

A concession I wanted to grab onto. Instead, I answered her question. "We live in hide tents when we travel and in wooden homes when we remain with the voxes in the mountains. The mountains are . . . glorious." I grinned, remembering. "The valley spreads before you, so vast, it makes your throat clench tight. But the desert has its own beauty. Whenever I step out of my hide home, something about it grabs me by the soul. It's in my blood, my bones, and I can't imagine living anywhere else."

"I haven't seen it before," she said in a wistful tone. "Maybe one day, I will."

"I'm going to," Brunnen said.

She huffed. "I thought you wanted to live in the village with me."

"I will for a time, but then I might travel to stay with Turren." His needy gaze met mine. "If I'm welcome."

"You will always have a place by my fire." This was an orc expression commonly made to a friend. In many ways, Brunnen already felt like a brother, and that pleased me immensely.

"Then expect me soon." Brunnen poked a tree trunk, and a branch snapped down to smack him on the head. He pinwheeled backward, dropping his staff, and gazed up at the tree in awe.

"See?" I said to Kaila. "Some trees are sentient."

"That's . . ." Brunnen plucked his spear off the ground and bowed to the tree. "I apologize. I'll be more respectful." With that, he kept walking, his step almost dancing across the ground.

"I've heard the desert is completely barren," Kaila said. "There's no water. No vegetation."

As a gardener, that must sound like a wasteland to my pretty mate.

"We live near oases where there's plenty of water."

"You do like to swim and bathe."

"The pools are beautiful, such a stark contrast to the dry sand stretching for cliks in all directions. It's hot during the day, which makes the pools welcome, but it cools down nicely at night. Then, we slumber beneath thick blankets within our snug homes."

"You mentioned Brunnen being welcome at your fire, so you must burn . . . something."

"In the mountains, wood. In the desert, dung."

Her eyes widened. "Poop? You cook food over poop?"

Put that way, I'd be incredulous myself.

"It's not *our* dung. The voxes provide plenty, as do

other creatures living in the sand. And we don't cook food over it. We use it for our central fire in the evening when everyone gathers."

"What fuel do you use to cook food, then?"

"The desert is dry, but plants find a way to grow. We dry those and use them. And we have ovens at the oasis."

"Like the stoves we used in the village fueled by wood. I can't picture a place with almost no water. Sand everywhere."

"As I said, it's beautiful. Treacherous at times, but so is the forest."

"And my village," she said softly. "How do you find enough to drink? I assume there are no rivers."

"You're correct. When we travel, we carry water, but there are plants we cut and smash to release their juices. There's nothing sweeter or tastier than that." Except her, my precious Kaila.

Anticipation coiled across my bones. I couldn't wait until tonight when we'd be alone.

CHAPTER 15
KAILA

I had a dilemma. I was starting to care for Turren, yet I still ached to be free from anyone who'd place demands on my time and body. When my brother and I fled the village, I'd looked forward to joining up with the women and starting a new life.

Now I kept picturing the desert world Turren described and seeing myself there—with him.

How could I decide what I wanted?

Tomorrow, we'd reach the village, and I'd need to choose. Did I dare change the course of my life for a male I only met a few days ago?

As darkness started to gobble up the sunlight, we stopped and gathered wood for a fire.

"I'll go hunt," Turren said softly. His gaze fell on Brunnen. "Will you protect your sister while I'm away?"

"I will." Brunnen's chest puffed, and he brandished his staff. "She'll be safe with me."

I would be, which is a funny thought. A few days ago, I was my brother's protector, not the other way around. In a short time, Brunnen had changed from the young boy slowly growing into the man he'd one day be into someone with confidence. Determination. He was incredibly brave.

"If you'll give me a blade, I can protect myself," I said dryly, not wanting to make my brother feel bad, but he was only thirteen. Taller than me already, but in many ways still a child.

"Will this do?" Turren slid a medium-length blade from the sheath at his waist and held it toward me, hilt-first.

"Yes." I flashed him a smile. It seemed all I wanted to do when he was around was grin.

I wasn't falling in love.

I was *in like*.

My growl slipped out. "My feelings are not changing."

Brunnen huffed. "Kaila." Shaking his head, he turned and started toward the river not far away. "I'm going to go bathe." He grabbed his bag with the clothing I'd washed and hung to dry the night before and stomped over to the bank, where he hung the bag on a low branch.

"I'm not trying to change you," Turren said softly, nudging the blade toward me again.

I took it and held it by my side. "That's not what I meant."

His head tilted. "Then what *did* you mean?"

"I feel as if nothing in my life is stable, and that's a complete betrayal."

"In what way?"

"When my parents died, I promised my little brother I'd be there for him, that I'd provide him with a home and stability. Yet, here I am, dragging him through the forest. You described your home, how you move from one location to another, how you don't care about possessions. But I do."

"Things don't make the person."

That didn't make any sense. "Don't you see? My life—Brunnen's life—is in complete turmoil. I abandoned the only home I've ever known, which some would call foolish. It wasn't much, but it provided the stability we both needed. But, no, I left it. Walked right out the door as if it meant nothing. Someone else will move in and claim it. My parents worked hard to make it nice for us. It was the only legacy they left us. It was a home, and I tossed it aside. For what?" I waved my arm toward the pile of wood we'd use to cook our meal. "We have nothing. All my work, all these years to provide for Brunnen, and we have nothing! We still have to hunt and prepare and cook the food, all while hoping wild creatures don't attack and kill us. Then we'll sleep in a tree. A tree! That isn't a home. It isn't stability, the one thing I crave above all else."

"You keep stating this is about giving Brunnen what he needs, but have you asked him what he wants?"

"Of course he wants what I provide for him. A home. Food on the table. A future. Right now, he has nothing but a staff and a few pieces of clothing." My eyes stung with tears, but they were generated by frustration and self-loathing, not true anger with Turren.

"Do you think a building and food make a person happy?"

"It's much easier to be happy when you have things than when you don't."

"Is it?"

"You don't understand. You live the life of a wanderer." I shuddered, though even I had to admit, if only to myself, that his life sounded free and compelling. "You don't know from one moment to the next where you'll sleep or what you'll eat. How can that make you happy?"

He tapped his chest. "Because I carry my home and my happiness here," His arm swept out, "I don't expect the world around me to bring me joy. I find it within myself."

"It's not possible to be happy with nothing."

"It is. You just need to see it."

Yet, I couldn't. "I've made a mistake."

"In leaving the village? Tell me now, and we'll turn around. I'll take you back, and I'll not only bring you to the fortress gate, but I'll also go inside with you. If someone thinks to steal your home from you, I'll help you take it back. If you wish to live elsewhere, I'll be there beside you, helping you find that place."

"You'd do something like that for me?" The notion did something to me, making my bones melt and my heart thump faster. "Why?"

"Because I want to help you."

"Is it really that simple?" And was that the only reason?

"Few things are ever simple, though I'm sure you've learned that already. I told you that you're my fated mate. That I will love you until the day I die and beyond."

"That's the fates talking." Reaching up, I flicked his pendant that blazed even now. "It's this thing, not you. Not the real you inside."

"Do you think I believe solely because of my pendant?" So much emotion cratered his voice, his face. It wrenched my heart right out of my chest. "I feel this way because I've come to know you."

"You can't," I whispered.

"I can." His face darkened, and I found such despair in his eyes. "You're *everything* I need. Everything I'll ever want. You're the spark in my heart, the surge of power in my blood. With you, I'm more than just Turren, more than just an orc male doing his best to please his people with this." He thrust his scarred arm between us.

"How did it happen? You didn't say."

"That doesn't matter."

"I think it does."

"Because you think it makes me a lesser male?" He shook his head.

"No. Because I think it makes you a better one."

His sigh bled out. "When I was very young, a creature in the mountains where my parent's clan made their home grabbed me. It nearly killed me. I was left with this." He twisted his arm, showing off the network of scars. "I was told this made me weak. I was told I'd never be a full male. But I tell you right now, I am."

"I'm sorry." Here I was, floundering around with my emotions when Turren had something so horrible happen to him. It had impacted his entire life.

"If you reject me," he said softly, returning his arm to his side. "I'll go on. I'm much too strong to do anything else. As I said, my clan needs me, and I have so much of myself to give." He gripped my shoulders tight, his gaze full of passion. I couldn't look away. His voice lowered to a whisper. "Yet without you, I'm nothing. Not inside, where it matters most." Turning, he stalked away. He stopped at the edge of the clearing and remained motionless, staring toward the water.

I wanted to go to him, wrap my arms around him, and tell him . . . what? I wished I knew, then I could find the words to tell him everything within *me*. But when my parents died, and I shed the carefree girl I'd been and donned the mantle of a woman, mother, and provider, I'd lost my voice. I'd suppressed it.

And I wasn't sure I could bring that person, that voice, back to the surface again.

"I don't want to go back." Utter defeat made my shoulders curl forward. For one moment, I felt as if I was giving up already, turning away from a battle I hadn't yet fought. But that was silly. Turren and I weren't enemies.

Yet we weren't lovers either.

"I just need time to decide if I want to go forward on the path I've chosen," I said. Or if I needed to consider something new.

He turned and walked back to stand in front of me, in control of his emotions once more. If only I could calm the turmoil inside myself.

Suppress it, I supposed.

"If that's the case," he said. "Then you have some time yet. You need to decide what you want for your future. I believe you left your village because you wanted a new life. Money is a physical thing. So is a building. Even food. They're not things you can truly hold on to. In the desert, we have nothing but what we can carry and what's held in our hearts. One could say we're poor because we don't clutter up our lives with possessions. But they're wrong. We always have each other. That's the true value in life, not a roof overhead or food on the table. Yes, we carry weapons. We hunt. We move from one place to another and at each destination, we settle back into the life we left behind. Our buildings wait for us with tight bags full of possessions. But none of that has true value. None of it is real."

"That doesn't make sense. Of course it's real." I lifted the blade. "*This* is real."

"Is it?" He tapped my chest. "In here, is the home your parents lived in real? The food you fed your brother while he was growing? Or do you carry what's most important inside your heart already?"

"There's nothing in my heart. I closed it off when my parents died. It hurts too much to care."

"You love Brunnen. I see it in your eyes, in every gesture. You cannot deny this."

"I do love him."

Only him?

"This is about more than Brunnen, more than a building and food," he said. "This is about us."

Us? There was no us. I couldn't let this male into my life. "You're making me feel things!"

"Then you're living." He said it earnestly; I could feel it, warmth on my very soul.

"I don't want to live if it means feeling like this," I said, trying to make him understand. "I'm being consumed alive by rushes of joy when . . ." I couldn't name it out loud. Rushes of joy when he was near. I wanted to touch him. An enormous wave of water was threatening to drown me because I knew . . . I *knew* . . . that tomorrow I'd have to tell him goodbye.

And that was what this came down to. To give my brother what he needed, I'd have to lose . . .

No, don't name it, I chided myself.

But the feeling kept cresting within me before sliding back again. If I remained with Turren much longer, it would burst into view and then I'd have to own the fact that I was falling in love.

"Don't you see?" His words were tender, like his fingers gliding down my face. His gaze was no longer focused on me but on the ground—or inward. "You left everything tangible behind. So much waits for you in the future if you're willing to grab onto it and hold it close. This is a chance to be the person you've always wanted to be."

"Who is that woman?" I started pacing in front of him while he watched me with gentleness in his eyes. It smacked me in the chest, in that place that had spasmed since my parents were killed. My ribs ached, and my heart hurt even more. "I don't believe I know her any longer."

"Give her time." His smile rose, but it was crooked. "She's waiting for you."

With that, he melted into the woods.

CHAPTER 16
TURREN

What could I say to my mate to ease her pain? She carried such burdens. If only she could see that I'd gladly share them with her.

I thought three days was enough, yet I was too confident, too sure in the mate bond. With orcs, a mating like this was a blessing. Both welcomed it. Who wouldn't be happy that the fates made sure the person you'd love most entered your life?

Yet humans didn't have bonds like this, not with each other.

I knew they could find a mate bond with orcs. I'd seen it with my friends and their human mates. They adored each other so much it hurt to watch them together. I'd felt envy, pain being with them, yet it also brought joy because in my heart, I knew I only needed to find *my* mate, and I'd share the same wonder.

Now I'd found her, and she couldn't decide if she wanted me.

As I moved through the forest, seeking food to supplement the fish Brunnen would catch for our dinner, I clutched my pendant.

It blazed.

"The fates are not wrong. I must trust in this. I need to remain patient."

Yet it hurt.

But pain was a fleeting thing, much like the possessions Kaila believed had the most value. Pain could be thrust aside in a moment. I'd done it once, when everything in my life had fallen apart.

Love did this.

What would I do if Kaila rejected me tomorrow?

Shaking my head, I put that aside for now. It was unwise to walk in the woods while distracted. My focus needed to remain on hunting and seeking food. Watching out for predators. And making sure I returned to my mate and her brother unharmed.

I still had tonight to win my mate's love. She'd responded to my touch today, though that was a physical thing, not of the heart.

Or was it? Perhaps her body was telling me what her heart was too frightened to voice aloud.

That gave me hope and the strength I needed.

I picked berries and came across a tree with globules the size of my hand that, when cooked, were slightly spicy and very tasty. I collected an armload, placing them in the large pouch I'd brought with me.

I thought of setting snares, but we didn't have far to travel tomorrow before we reached the village, and we wouldn't need the meat the snares might provide.

Returning to the camp, I walked to the river, smiling to see Kaila and her brother cleaning fish. I lit the fire and placed the globules nearby to roast in the coals. Then I took a packet of well-ground grain mix from my larger pouch and mixed it with the berries. I'd fry the cakes and we could eat them for breakfast as we walked toward the village.

Kaila and her brother walked up from the river, joining me, and while Kaila didn't give me the smile I ached for, her gaze met mine. I saw a calmness there that reassured me.

We ate, enjoying the food, and cleaned up after.

"I'm going to find a tree," Brunnen said. "I'm tired." His attention fell on me, and he closed one eye quickly before opening it again and giving me a subtle smile. Did he have something in his eye? That was a cause for distress, not smiling.

"Are you alright?" I asked.

"I am."

Hmm. "Would you like help selecting your tree?"

"No, I can do it. I know how to find them now, and what to avoid."

"Let me know if you can't locate one." I stood. "I'll be glad to help."

With a nod and a frown sent Kaila's way, Brunnen strode into the woods with his staff ready for defense.

"He's growing up fast," Kaila said mournfully. "It seems like yesterday he was a tiny boy nestling in my arms."

"He's a strong warrior already. Brave and loyal." Especially to his sister, who he clearly adored.

"He is," she said with a sigh.

"Would you like to bathe in the river before it gets too dark?" I nudged my head to the bag with our clothing, though mine consisted only of loincloths.

"Yes." She went to the bag and pulled out clean things.

Grabbing onto my bag and my hope, I followed her toward the river.

CHAPTER 17
KAILA

I still hadn't gotten used to seeing him so . . . naked. So virile.

He exuded power and a sensuality I hadn't found in any other male. I sensed I would never find it in someone again and that cut me deeply.

I'd always thought orcs were monsters. Now I knew they were people with deep feelings, incredible strength, and intelligence—at least Turren was.

I still wasn't sure what might happen tonight, if anything. No, what I wanted to happen. Except that I was going to kiss him. I needed to feel his mouth on mine before it was too late. A real kiss, not the peck on the lips I'd given him last night.

At the riverbank, we hung our clean clothing over a low branch.

"I'll swim downriver?" he said. "I'll stay close enough you can call out if you have need."

What if my need had nothing to do with danger?

"Thank you," I said softly.

I kept thinking about the thrust of his fingers inside me, the way he'd placed his mouth between my legs and sucked. His tongue.

I'd had a taste, and my body wanted the full meal. But what about my mind and my heart? Stupid body parts couldn't get in sync with each other.

He strode along the shore and when he was far enough away he must think I couldn't see him, he started untying his loincloth.

I should pay attention to removing my own things, to getting into the water and bathing, but all I could do was stare.

I'd seen naked men before. I'd been intimate with a few. When I was with the two men back at the village, they'd made no effort to hide while they removed their clothing. And they, like many men I knew, were muscled from hard work. Few had the luxury of paying others to do things for them. They did it themselves and that made for a lean, well-muscled body, my own included.

But none of the men I'd seen came even close to the beauty of Turren's form. He'd been sculpted by the very fates themselves, from his thick horns to his broad chest, to his narrow hips tapering down his legs. His arm . . . only added to his beauty. Did he know that?

He finished unwinding his loincloth and tossed it

aside. He couldn't be aware I watched or he'd . . . hide? Actually, I doubted Turren would ever be one to hide, though he wouldn't flaunt himself.

He behaved naturally, bending forward to do something with his bare foot.

With his legs spread wide enough I could see between them, I gaped at the view of his balls and his massive cock. How did he fit that inside a woman? It would rip her apart.

Yet my body loosened. The low punch of warmth in my belly feathered down to pool between my legs, to make me wet as if Turren was with me, touching me like he had today. My body appeared more than willing to welcome that thick, long cock. It would relish the experience, shoving groans of pleasure up my throat while I clung to him, begged him for more.

He pivoted and strode down into the water, giving me another view of his cock. It hung loosely, not erect like it had been each morning when we slept together on a branch.

When he splashed into the water and groaned, my body spiraled. More wetness gushed between my legs. It was a simple sound one might make in pleasure. His groan hadn't been sexual. He wasn't making the sound because he was savoring my taste or the feel of my body responding to his touch.

"Undress," I snarled to myself. "Get in the water."

I mechanically removed my clothing, setting them aside to be washed after I'd finished. When I entered the river, I muffled my sigh of pleasure. I gave thanks that the chilly water cooled the heat building inside me. I washed and floated, allowing my body to drift with the current until I reached Turren. I wasn't doing this to get close to him. I wanted to talk, to learn more about him.

"Would you ever want to live in one place at a time?" I asked, treading water to remain with him.

He dipped his legs down to do the same. "No."

"That's it, a simple no?" Why did I feel betrayed by his answer?

"I'm not an orc who can be tied down. If I stayed in one place, I'd have to shackle myself to a job. I wouldn't be free."

And that would be a true crime. I could see that now.

But how did a woman who craved stability build a bridge to a male who had wandering forged in his bones?

I'd said something wrong, and I wasn't sure how to fix things between us. Again, I counseled patience. We had tonight and tomorrow morning, and I wasn't wasting one second.

I turned away while she left the water, walked up to where she'd left her things, and dressed. Then I did the same, joining her by the dying fire after I'd donned my loincloth.

"Are you ready to scale a tree?" I asked, my voice croaking. Emotions were a tough thing. They kept tangling with my sense of duty, and I wasn't sure how to unscramble them.

"Yes." We walked into the woods, and I studied the trees, finally selecting one. At her nod, I lifted her into my arms and quickly made my way up into the canopy, where I settled on the wide branch.

She climbed into my lap, facing me, looking up at

me while her fingertips stroked my arms. If she kept doing that, my cock was going to wake up and demand attention. I doubted that was where she wanted to take things tonight.

I lifted my pendant and asked a thin branch to descend to hold my whisp lantern. Once I'd hung it, it swayed softly, making light dance around us.

"It still feels magical," she whispered. "We had whisp lanterns back in the village, but somehow, out here in the wild, they feel different."

"What do you enjoy doing most in the world?" I asked, craving to hear her voice and whatever she might wish to tell me.

She smiled up at me. "I enjoyed reading, but I think my favorite thing was working in the soil, growing things."

"Flowers?" I asked.

"And vegetables. There's something satisfying about placing a seed in the moist soil and watching it sprout. Then carefully feeding the new growth until it's big enough to produce something you can eat. And when you eat it, you can separate the seeds and start the process all over again. It's a never-ending circle that soothes me."

"Some of my clan grow grains and vegetables near the oasis where we spend our winter months. While it's often hot in the desert, the water chills the air enough we can sleep at night."

"You mentioned hide houses?"

"We tan the skins and maintain them when we're there, but many times, it's nice to sleep out under the stars."

"I didn't do that in the village. I saw the stars but only in passing at night. Most of the time, it was good to be inside before it got dark. It wasn't always safe going out at night. Inside, with whisp lanterns lit, it was cozy. Welcoming. A home."

"You'll have the same feeling of security in the new village. I've met the caedos and her mate, and they're both strong and honest. Everyone there has worked hard to build homes and the fortress walls."

"Even there, they need walls?"

"Walls protected you from the shaydes and ashenclaws when you lived in your village, as did the walls of your home."

"That's true. I guess I thought that there, they wouldn't need them. That they could leave their homes and wander about in safety."

"They have guards. No one has been killed by a shayde or ashenclaw."

Yet. No place was completely safe. Our world could too easily be shaken, broken.

"Tell me more about the desert."

"You wish to hear about it?"

"I want to try to see why you love it, why you enjoy that life so much you can't imagine living any other way."

How could I find the right words to impress her?

"You'd think that with all the openness and with the vast sky above, there wouldn't be much to look at, but the way the sun cuts across the sky in the early morning is stunning." There were my words again, slipping easily from my tongue. When my emotions were involved, my body could sing. "Soft pinks, golds, and oranges paint the very air. And in the evening, when the sun sets, the sky is ablaze with red and orange so vivid, your heart feels ready to soar up there and grab onto the beams."

I looked down at her, smiling because she listened raptly. "If I could, I'd bunch them up and gift them to you. A sun bouquet whose beauty would only be surpassed by yours."

Her breath caught. "It sounds pretty, much prettier than me."

"When I first saw you, I felt as if everything shifted inside me, like I had been walking a path that was good enough for then but nowhere near as wonderful as it could be with you beside me."

"You say the sweetest things."

"I mean them."

"Your desert sounds beautiful."

"As I said, there are dangers there, but we're not held back by walls. We've found ways to lessen the danger, so many walk at night, lay on the ground to look at the stars, and even sleep out in the open."

"It does sound freeing."

Did I hear longing in her voice?

"I'd love to show it to you one day. Share it with you. Our mountain home, too, that's so different."

"Maybe someday." Her face scrunched. "Why else do you love the desert?"

"It's beautiful in a fierce, raw way. The sand is always shifting, forming new peaks or being smoothed by the wind. Every time you look, it's a new painting, and each is prettier than the last. There are no pretenses out there. I've never felt as alive as I do when I'm walking in the sand. There's peace, a solitude that sinks into your bones. It renews you each time you take a step."

I could tell she was trying to understand.

I'd told her I couldn't leave my clan, my duties. It was more that I didn't want to.

Did she realize that if she asked, if she offered a place with her anywhere, I'd choose her every time? I'd mourn the loss of my desert and mountain homes, of my friends and the people I'd loved since I found them.

Without her, nothing else mattered.

I couldn't tell her that, couldn't put my feelings into words that would make her understand. If she wanted to be with me, she'd tell me.

"What about the mountains?" she asked. "I've never been higher than this tree. Why do you like living there?"

"There, we've built homes into the side of the mountains. We can walk from the back of our homes into vast caverns with pools. The voxes breed and lay their seeds there."

"What else?" Her voice sounded sleepy.

"I'm boring you."

She tapped my chest. "Not one bit. Tell me."

"When you're up in the hills, you can see for many cliks. The rich valleys, the other mountain peaks. And so many trees. We have a forest like this one, but it's different."

"Maybe I *could* see it one day."

I'd wait forever for that moment.

My longing for her was so sharp, I felt the cut all the way to my bones. She was the light calling me home and the cusp of a new day full of wonder. Every bit of her roared through me.

I couldn't imagine not being with her, seeing her, touching her. And soon, the time might come when I'd need to accept that no matter what I did, no matter what I said, she'd turn away.

What I offered wouldn't be enough.

Pain stabbed through me.

It was all I could do to suck in a breath.

It was all my heart could do to keep beating.

CHAPTER 19

KAILA

When Turren described his desert and mountain homes, I tried to picture them. It was hard when all I could see was the forest around us, the canopy above, and the dense vegetation below. I'd lived all my life in the village with the woods looming around us. I'd played on the edge of the forest under the watchful eyes of my parents, and I'd dared to venture to the river sometimes to swim and fish. Everything in my world could be seen and touched if I stretched out my hand.

But a desert? Vast mountains and deep valleys? I couldn't imagine living in places like that. Wide open spaces might frighten me. The height of the mountains might scare me. How would I hide from danger if there were no trees, no fortress walls, no tiny home to escape into? And caves? Creatures might lurk within them.

He mentioned dangers I couldn't imagine, and the thought of facing the unknown made me feel exposed and vulnerable.

A part of me, what I called my adventurous Kaila, the one who would sometimes sneak to the river at sunset and dance through the shallow water, that Kaila ached to see these places Turren loved above all others. To take a chance at a life I've never imagined.

Could I find the strength to go places like that?

I wouldn't be alone. While I could suggest I travel there with him to see the desert or the mountains, to experience them with him, he would see that as me choosing him. I couldn't do that until I was sure I would never turn back.

I . . . cared for him a lot already. Battling with him had shown me how patient he was. Watching him with my brother showed how kind. And touching him showed me how he could light my very body on fire.

He said we were fated to be together, and I could tell he believed that to his very soul.

Did I?

I swallowed, but there was a lump in my throat that wouldn't go down no matter how hard I tried to force it. It hurt almost as much as my chest. I'd only known him for a few days. Was that long enough to know if I wanted to be with him forever? Saying yes to the questions in his eyes meant taking a chance, thrusting myself out into the open, into a place that, for a person who craved stability, could be considered a nightmare.

I did know one thing. I had tonight with him and tomorrow morning. I'd have to decide when we reached the village. But I didn't have to make that decision right now. Perhaps, for once, I should live in the moment without worrying about what might come next.

And this moment was for Turren.

"You're thinking," he said softly. "Perhaps, instead, you should be sleeping."

I could taste the vulnerability, the uncertainty in his voice.

He was beautiful in a foreign way, and already dear. How had I gone from snarling at him to finding him so perfect it made my lungs ache?

I focused on his mouth. I'd kissed him the night before, but it was quick, fleeting. I'd barely felt it. I wanted to know what it was like to kiss someone that only in my wildest dreams could belong to me.

No, not just someone. *Turren.*

I was beginning to believe there wasn't anything I wouldn't do to taste his mouth, to feel his body pressed against mine. My skin burned at the thought of letting all my inhibitions go. My heart thundered loudly in anticipation. Everyone in the forest must hear it.

"Have I stolen the words from your mouth, my

bold mate?" he asked, a touch of humor in his voice. "Usually it was me who can't find them."

"You speak so eloquently."

And even when it was clear he was as uncertain about where this was going as me, he could still find a way to laugh.

What would it be like to stand by the side of this male for the rest of my days?

"How can you call me bold?" I asked, still staring at his mouth.

"Look at you. You left the village."

"I told you why. We had to leave."

"You stepped away from everything that kept your feet solidly on the ground. While the world shifts now beneath you, and you're facing the unknown, you're still strong and determined."

"I've survived because of that determination."

"And I admire it very much."

"I want to kiss you." The words blurted out, cutting through the chitchat that was merely a distraction from the heat swirling around us.

His lips curled up before smoothing, and his eyes smoldered. They dropped to my mouth. "Then perhaps you should do so."

His lips were a bit plumper on the bottom and dark green, not that the color or shape mattered. I didn't care about anything like that. What mattered most to me about a person was who they were at their core, and I already admired everything about the person I'd found in Turren.

An undeniable need made me quiver. I could take what I needed for the night and decide what I wanted in the morning, or I could nudge him aside and continue . . .

Hiding.

That's what I was doing. I had no problem admitting that to myself. There was comfort in the stability I needed more than anything else.

Stop thinking. Start feeling.

Still focused on his mouth, I rose up onto my knees and slid my fingers across his shoulder to the nape of his neck. I stabbed my fingers through his hair, something I'd wanted to do almost from the moment I met him, though I would've denied the craving back then. I urged his face down to meet mine, for his mouth to find mine as I found his and all of him.

And we kissed. A real one this time, not the tease I'd given him before.

Like he'd dropped a spark onto me, and I was the tinder, I burst into flame. It consumed me like he was consuming my mouth.

My heart pounded with desire, and I latched onto his shoulders, clinging to him in the same way I wanted to cling to whatever he had to offer.

I might be scared about my uncertain future, but nothing frightened me now.

This. This was what I needed more than anything.

The feel of his mouth hungry on mine, the way his hands roamed my back before latching onto my arms and holding tight.

One hand slid to the nape of my neck and his fingers threaded into my hair, wrapping the strands around his palm and pressing to bring me closer. His other hand stroked along my jawline and teased down my neck to the top of my chest.

I moaned, pressing my breasts against him. He was made up of vast, warm flesh, and even if it took me a lifetime, I wanted to touch and taste it all.

Heat coiled up my spine, tightening and releasing, and I angled my head and parted my lips, inviting him to explore further.

His tongue dipped inside and glided across mine. He tasted like the herb he'd used to cleanse his teeth, a mix of mint and something wild. Our tongues entwined like I ached to be entwined with him.

With a groan, his mouth pressed down harder. His hand released my hair and slid down my back, pushing my lower body against his rigid cock. A thrill shot through me that I could drive him wild with such a simple touch. Drive myself wild too.

I tightened my legs around him and rocked my pelvis against his while he met me with furious vigor. His thick staff moved between my legs perfectly, sliding up to rub my clit with each thrust.

His mouth left mine only to trail across my jawline, and he delivered kisses, each one slow and with incredible care. As if he wanted to brand me with each and each had to be better than the one before.

With a quick thrust, he brought my blouse up over my head, and I almost laughed when he took the time to lay it gently across the branch holding our whisp lantern.

Then his mouth was on mine again, drinking and stroking while his warm hands glided from my belly to my chest.

Arching my spine, I begged for him to touch, to do everything he wanted with my breasts. I'd give the world to feel it all.

I yanked and tugged on his hair, urging him lower, and he did as I asked, lifting my breast with his hand to offer it to his mouth. He flashed a tusk-filled smile at me before diving down and sucking my nipple into his mouth.

My moan jerked out of me, and I thrust my hips forward, rocking against his cock that only seemed to get thicker. Longer. Harder.

He stroked his tongue across my nipple then rolled it between his teeth, gentle yet with enough strength it sent bolts shooting from my breast to my groin. I cried out, giving into this moment. Him. Because there was no other place I wanted to be but in his arms, feeling his mouth on me, his hands roaming my over-heated flesh.

Leaving my breast, my nipple puckered and wanting, he moved to the other. "My passionate mate. My beautiful mate. My perfect mate."

When he sucked the other nipple into his mouth, sensations rocked through my core. I frantically rubbed against him, everything building inside me to the point I was going to explode.

He lifted his head and gave me a crooked grin full of confidence laced with a hint of vulnerability. The latter endeared him to me to a point where I couldn't imagine why I had doubts.

For now, I shoved those doubts aside. They were for daylight. Tomorrow, which felt like a lifetime away.

He eased me down onto the wide branch, and his gaze slid from my mouth to my breasts and lower. With his gaze locked on mine, he trailed his knuckles around each nipple before moving lower. Lower. Until he came to the waistband of my skirt.

"I want to taste you. Will you let me, my precious mate?" he rasped, his voice hoarse with emotion.

Sanity tried to crowd into my mind, telling me I was uncertain about him, of this situation, of everything, but I stomped it flat and nodded.

With my legs splayed to the sides, he bunched up my skirt, dragging it slowly higher. I lifted my hips to let him move it away. A few tugs, and my undergarment was gone, joining my blouse or fluttering toward the ground. I didn't know, and I didn't care. All I wanted and needed was to *feel*.

While his mouth returned to my breast, his tongue

gliding across my nipple, he stroked my thighs in broad circles. Each loop brought his hand closer to my core, to the place where everything had coiled tight. I wasn't sure I could stand it.

He parted my thighs and when his fingers glided through my wetness, my moan roared up my throat. I rocked my hips up to meet his hand as he ran one finger over my clit. Others slid inside my passage, stroking my inner walls in a way destined to drive me out of my mind with pleasure.

"You're so beautiful and perfect," he said, leaving my breast and punctuating his words with kisses across my belly. His fingers slid deeper within me, coated with my wetness, my saturated need for his touch. "I can't imagine how the fates could decide I was worthy of the exquisite joy I might find in your arms." He hitched first one of my legs, then the other, onto his shoulders and looked up at me, his fingers stilling. "I'm going to do all I can to show them and you that they made no mistake, that what we have is sublime."

This male said the prettiest things. Did the dirtiest things to my body.

And I wanted more.

As if he heard my words, though I hadn't spoken aloud, he gave me a quick grin.

Then his head burrowed between my thighs.

"All day long, I've ached to be with you like this," I growled against her wet folds. I pumped my fingers deeper within her. "Touch you like this again. Taste you. If I could feast on you, I'd never need food or water again."

She sucked in her breath, but she didn't snarl or try to back away. She relaxed into my touch; her hands tentatively reached down to stroke my horns. "I've never had anyone do . . . this before. I'm not sure how it will feel."

"Let me show you." While still moving my fingers within her, I licked from her entrance to her clit with jerky snarls erupting from my throat. I was greedy, and she tasted sweet, like sunshine. Warmth. Need. I'd never get enough.

I found her clit and licked it in long swaths, dragging my tongue back and forth across it while it tightened and thickened, shouting out her arousal. She gasped and latched onto my horns. Shockwaves blasted from my sensitive horns to my cock, and it stiffened even further. It ached. *I* ached. I'd do anything to be able to love her like this every day. To claim her fully even if only once.

"I'm a starving male," I growled as I continued to love her clit, a part of her as exquisite as the rest. She was exquisite, so plump and lush. She was made for me. My cock, my mouth, and my soul. "Give every-thing to me."

She was lost, her head thrashing on the branch, her hands alternating between tugging on my horns and pushing down to keep my mouth on her body.

Her thighs clenched my head, and she writhed, arching up to meet my fingers, the strokes of my tongue on her clit.

Her cries rang out, sending pleasure to my very soul. I was going to eat her like this all through the night, drinking from her while bringing her to one peak after another. If all I had was now, I'd make it last as long as I could. I'd make sure by morning she knew she was mine.

My pendant blazed, lighting up the wetness between my pretty mate's legs, her swollen flesh, and the way her body took my fingers so well. I added more, feeling the stretch followed by the give as she surrendered.

Her keening cry rang out, startling the world

around us, similar to prey being devoured by a predator. My chest rumbled with my growl, and I slowed my fingers, coiling them, twisting them, stretching them. Her inner walls trembled, and her clit tightened. She'd give me what I craved most soon, her endless pleasure, and I was going to drink it down. Swallow all of her whole.

When she came, she did it so beautifully, my eyes stung. I wasn't a male who cried. I hadn't done so for many years.

Yet I did now as my mate gave into bliss.

And when her eyes locked on mine, I could see a future there for us both.

I prayed to the fates it would come true.

CHAPTER 21
KAILA

I lay splayed wide on the branch in complete abandon. While my hands continued to stroke his horns, he moved his fingers within me at a slower pace, bringing me back down to this world slowly.

When he pulled them out, my body made a greedy, sucking sound that should make the heat of embarrassment turn me scarlet. But how could I be ashamed of what we'd done? It was sublime. Utterly perfect.

And I wanted him to do it again.

But that was the problem. *Again* would turn into more, and before I knew it, I'd be agreeing to almost anything as long as he promised never to stop.

I still wasn't sure where I belonged. At the village or taking on the dangers and uncertainty of a new life by his side.

So I said nothing as he helped me dress, as he

tugged me onto his lap and into his arms. His cock was a stiff pole between us, and I itched to cup it, stroke it, to give him even a fraction of the pleasure he'd shown me.

"Sleep," he said before I could lift his loincloth and begin. "I want to hold you all night. Touch and taste you again if you'll let me."

"Yes." I could only breathe that one word. I was so enthralled by him I couldn't say no. Was this what it would always be like between us?

The thought scared me when it should thrill me.

Again, I shoved aside my feelings both for him and for what I might want for my future. Here and now was what mattered, and I was going to drink it in and hold it tight for as long as I could.

I drifted to sleep with him rubbing my back. And woke to the long stroke of his hands up and down my back. His cock prodded between us, urgent and thick, and this time, I didn't hesitate. I lifted his loincloth, letting his cock spring out. A part of me gulped. He was incredibly large. How could something this enormous fit within my body?

But we weren't going to do that tonight. I couldn't until I was sure. It wouldn't be fair to either of us because after that, there would be no turning back.

While I stroked his cock, my fingers barely meeting around it, he watched me.

His purr rumbled in his chest as his sleepy gaze

studied my face and my hand before he locked his eyes on mine once more.

My blood simmered, and low heat coiled down from my belly to between my legs once more. Pleasing him made me eager to feel his touch again.

His arms tightened around me. He held me, cherishing me and the simple touch I was giving him. I wanted to give him a taste of what he'd given me hours ago, to spend as much of tonight with him in almost every way, to find out what it would be like to belong to Turren.

When I stroked my thumb across the tip of his cock, gliding it through his wetness, he sucked in a breath.

His eyes smoldered with heat for me alone. What a heady feeling. A warmth that came from knowing that I could do this for him. Be the one he needed tonight.

While still pumping and stroking his cock, I tugged up my skirt, grateful I'd skipped wiggling around to dress in my undergarment as well. He had said we weren't through for the night. The last thing we needed was a barrier between us. Life was going to throw it up soon enough.

He slid his fingers beneath my blouse, cupping my breasts. He was so warm, so full of life. The heat of him sunk into my bones and simmered, making all of me come alive for the first time ever. Gone were thoughts of the other men I'd been with. None could or would ever compare to this male holding me now.

He rolled my nipples between his thumbs and fingers while I shifted back and forth to bring the rest of my skirt up around my waist. I locked my heels on his hips and tilted back while milking his cock, tugging it up hard to his grunts and groans of bliss.

It had nubs on the sides, and they vibrated. I could only imagine how that would feel if he was thrusting inside me, driving them against my inner walls until all I could feel was him.

"What's this?" I asked when my hand brushed against something else.

He grinned sleepily, lazily, so full of passion it nearly overwhelmed me. I turned my gaze down, studying the smaller cock thrusting against his abs.

"You have two?" I asked.

"That's my spur. Your spur when you want it."

"I don't know what a spur was." But oh, yes, did I ever want it. Once, twice. As many times as I could take it.

Danger lay in that direction, but I couldn't seem to drag my mind away from the world it was picturing. Fantasizing, actually, and all about him.

"When I ride you, my curious mate," he said, "my spur will find your clit and give it special attention."

Fates help me. I was drowning in Turren. His words, the feel of his cock thrusting against my hand as his hips rocked us upward, and now the thought of this second cock attending to my clit.

"Watch," he said, his groan biting out when I

touched a particularly sensitive part of his cock.

The second one stretched out, unerringly finding my clit. The tip latched on and began sucking, pumping my clit like I did his cock.

My eyes rolled back in my head, and I leaned backward, splaying my body wide to accept everything. May the fates keep his spur on my clit forever.

I melted against him, completely losing track of everything but bucking up against his spur.

"You're so beautiful. Touch me. Yes, like that. Give in to the pleasure my spur offers. It's yours. Always. Just like me."

His hand slipped between us, and he stroked his fingertips through my wetness. His spur continued to pulse against my clit, holding on as if its sole purpose in life was to bring me endless joy.

And maybe it was.

I could have this, take this, claim all of this as my own. I just had to trust . . .

My core started trembling. My entire body was trembling. I moved my hand faster while he groaned and jerked his hips up to meet me.

I was coming apart and for once in my life, I didn't care if I was scattered across the entire world as long as this male gathered up the pieces and brought me back together.

"I can't hold out," he rasped. "I . . ." His words dissolved into groans, and he moved faster. His spur sucked harder, in tune with his cock.

I'd never felt anything like this before.

The warmth in his eyes enfolded me. And when he tugged on my nipples, I shattered.

His hoarse cry rang out as he joined me in this moment of bliss.

That wasn't the last time we did anything that night. Sometime near dawn, he roused me with soft strokes between my legs. He laid my limp body on the branch and proceeded to eat me again.

I placed my heels on his shoulders and used them as leverage to buck up against his mouth.

And when he was finished, he leaned back, licked his lips and growled. "Again."

I woke with the sunrise and watched him sleep. He looked younger now, as if he shed all his cares when he finally let go.

I was glad I could give him pleasure last night, that I could share with him even a bit of what he'd given me.

My limp body coiled around his as if I never wanted to let go. In many ways, I didn't. Yet, in many ways, the thought of turning my back on the only security I'd ever known still scared me.

We'd reach the village today and then I'd make my decision.

I could only hope it was the right one.

CHAPTER 22
TURREN

A sharp cry awoke me, and I looked down at my mate, seeing the same concern mirrored in her eyes.

"What's . . .?" Her eyes widened when the hoarse sound echoed around us once more. "Brunnen."

Fear roared through me, and I sprung up with her in my arms. I held her as I leaped, flinging myself down from one branch to another, shielding her body from branches scraping against us from my rapid movement.

I stopped on the last branch and lowered her quickly to her feet, cupping her face, making her look up at me with her wild eyes full of so much fear it sliced into my guts with the heat of a hot blade.

"He will be all right," I said. "This I promise."

Another cry rang out.

She quivered, her fingers digging into my arms. "Please. Help him."

"Stay here."

I didn't wait for her nod. I only pressed her back against the trunk and made sure she was steady before I leaped off the branch and raced toward the area where I'd heard the scream. Guttural cries rang out ahead along with the chitter of at least one shayde. They rarely hunted during the day but rarely did not mean never. I wanted to bellow for him to hold on, that I was coming, but I couldn't let anything know I was on my way, that I was filled with a fierce resolve to slash and burn through everything to reach Brunnen.

I burst into a clearing and spied him standing near the edge, his back against a tree, his staff lifted.

Three shaydes surrounded him. If he could leap, he might be able to grab a branch above, though the odds weren't good that he'd find one. The slender tree hadn't grown tall enough to produce limbs that would support the youngling's weight.

Sunlight glinted off tears streaming down his face, but even in his fear, strength glistened in his eyes. They flicked to me.

"Stay away," he cried. "They'll hurt you. Get to Kaila. Keep her safe." Stark desperation came through in his voice. "I'll . . . hold them off. Protect her!"

One of the shaydes spun and started stalking toward me on its four legs ending in thick, sharp claws.

Its gleaming red eyes locked on me, revealing my imminent death. When it reached the middle of the meadow, light hit the enormous lizard creature, and its long, spiked tail swept furiously back and forth behind it. One beast would be a challenge for an orc warrior. Three?

If we were going to survive, I needed to be clever.

I stomped my foot, and a second shayde peeled away from Brunnen, joining the other that approached me like a predator with prey.

Something blurred past me, and my guttural groan rang out.

Kaila streaked toward the shaydes, waving her arms with one of my short blades in her hands. If willpower could take down the beasts, she'd do it. But she didn't stand a chance. She was soft, fragile, and nowhere near ready to take on this threat.

I rushed after her, putting myself between her and the shaydes while Brunnen cried out and slashed toward the remaining shayde with his staff.

The beast yelped and sprang backward, but I was too focused on the ones who'd noted Kaila's arrival and locked their eyes on fresh, more delicate prey.

"No." With a bellow, I leaped, springing over her and landing hard in front of her. She ran into my back. Her blade nicked my shoulder, but I barely felt the sting. I was too centered on what I'd need to do to protect my mate and her brother.

I'd die to make sure they made it out of this meadow alive.

The two shaydes rushed me from either side, and I swung out with my blade. It was knocked aside by the leathery hide of one of them and fell from my grip. Before I could pull another, the beast took advantage of my lack of defense, moving in closer. Saliva dripped from its fangs, and I saw my death in its eyes.

I would face it bravely.

They sprung on me at once, knocking into me.

Kaila's scream echoed around me, followed by Brunnen's hoarse cry.

More than anything, I wanted to save her. I needed to be the male she could proudly call her own. To give her everything I had inside me, then gather more together and hand that to her as well, along with my heart.

I was facing death too soon. Why was it always too late for a male like me?

Kaila . . .

I landed hard on my back with the beast on top of me, its claws scraping across my sides though not biting deep. Not yet, but soon.

I latched my fingers around its throat, squeezing, but its scaled hide was too thick, and the creature didn't even wheeze.

"Stop it." Kaila flailed against the beast, smacking it with bare hands, while the second sprung over the first and landed behind her. "No, please. Leave him alone."

"Run," I groaned. "Run!"

She continued hitting the shayde. I couldn't see Brunnen; couldn't hear him. Was he already dead?

It wasn't supposed to end like this. I was their protector, their guide to the village. I needed more time to show her . . .

The shayde's head snapped toward mine.

And it licked me.

Stunned, my grip slackened.

The shayde purred. A glance to my right showed the second nuzzling Kaila's back, also purring. While she remained frozen, her wide eyes filled with tears, it licked up her back, dragging her blouse along with it.

Then I remembered Taen. The shayde had stayed near my clan while Dakur's mate, Nia, recovered from her wound. The beast hadn't come close enough for me to interact with it, and after seeing it kill a man and rip him apart, I wasn't sure I wanted to get anywhere near it. Frightened themselves, my people were grateful. A creature like that didn't belong among us, though Dakur assured everyone the Taen wouldn't harm a teetser.

"What's happening?" Kaila sobbed.

I nudged the shayde aside and rose to my feet, taking her hand and pulling her into my arms.

Brunnen was still pressed back against the tree with the shayde standing in front of him, watching.

"Push it aside," I said, my heart a furious storm battering my ribs. "It won't harm you."

"Shayde," he shrieked. "Shayde!"

"These shaydes are . . . pets."

"That's not possible." Kaila pulled out of my arms, but she darted to the side. The two shaydes stood nearby, gazing at us with their tails sweeping back and forth. I expected them to leap on us, harm us, yet they almost appeared eager to play.

"My friend, Dakur, found three shayde kits when they were young. Their mother was killed, and they wouldn't have survived on their own. He took them to his clan here in the forest and raised them among the orcs. They're tame." Mostly. "Playful. And they won't harm us." They shouldn't, that is.

Did they hunt humans and orcs like all their brethren?

Kaila ran to her brother and put her arms around him, prying him away from the tree. They sidled around to the back and gazed at the shaydes with a mixture of awe and terror.

"Make them leave," Kaila cried out. "Please."

"I don't know how." I flipped my hands at them. "Go. Go away."

The shaydes continued to watch us, purring.

"I don't know any commands to make them do that," I said. "Come back. We need to gather our things and leave." I waited patiently while they hurried along the edge of the woods, staying as far as possible from the shaydes.

Other orc clans had made a treaty with the humans living in Kaila's village. In exchange for two human brides each year in the mate hunt, the orcs provided protection from shaydes and ashenclaws, another predator that hunted at night in packs. Kaila and Brunnen's fear of the shaydes was justified. For many years, humans had been killed by these creatures in the forest.

"Truly, they won't harm you," I said. May the fates make it so. "They're friends."

Brunnen wiped his eyes. He was brave and strong, but he was still on the cusp of being a child. Fear lurked in his eyes, but he darted a glance my way. "You're sure?"

As sure as I could be. "I assume some of my friends are in this area, perhaps visiting the village. The shaydes must've come with them."

"There are orcs about?" Kaila's wild gaze scanned the woods. "They won't hurt us, will they?"

"Of course not. Everyone in the woods is friendly."

"Except shaydes." A touch of fear came through in her voice. "And ashenclaws. I didn't think they'd come out during the day, that they only hunted at night."

"As I said, these three are friendly. They behave differently." I assumed they also hunted at night, though I wasn't going to mention that.

"Do you think I could touch one?" Curiosity had nudged aside Brunnen's fear. He strode over to stand beside me, watching the shaydes with a stunned expression and trembling hands.

"I believe so. Be cautious about it."

"Don't get near them," Kaila said shrilly. She remained by the woods, not coming closer.

"Turren says they're friendly," Brunnen said. "Haven't you ever wanted to touch one?"

"No." She swallowed, her gaze traveling from me to her brother and the shaydes. But she left the woods and came over to hover behind me, her hand on my lower back. I liked that she sought reassurance from me, but I didn't like the terror still lurking in her eyes. "Be careful, Brunnen. I don't like this."

I tugged her around in front of me and held her in the shelter of my arms.

Brunnen frowned our way before shrugging and turning back to the shaydes. "*How* do I touch them?"

"Let them sniff your fingers."

"They'll bite him," Kaila whimpered.

"I don't think they will."

"Think?" She huffed. "Please don't, Brunnen."

"You've spent most of your life protecting him, but I'm here now. Trust me in this?"

She looked up at me, so frightened and concerned. If only I could reassure her. "You're sure?"

"Look."

Her gasp rang out. "Brunnen . . ."

Her brother stood among the purring shaydes, carefully stroking one face, then another while the beasts gently nudged him.

"It's . . ." Kaila shook her head. "This isn't possible. Shaydes kill us. Eat us. They don't *lick* us."

"These do."

"I wonder how many other creatures could be friendly if they were raised by us?" Brunnen said. "Imagine. I've always thought the ashenclaws were beautiful. Such thick fur. And those eyes!"

"You haven't seen any ashenclaws except at a great distance," she said. "How do you know anything like that?"

"I used to go into the woods sometimes," he said with a lift of his chin.

"What? When?" She stepped toward him, scooting around the back of a shayde to approach him from behind, where she clung to his shirt. She watched the beasts who continued to lick and nuzzle Brunnen's belly.

"Not at night," he said.

"I didn't think so. You're always at home, safe with me."

"But when you were working, and I didn't have anything to do, I used to go to the woods to collect wood for the smithy shop or to look for tubers along the river. You like them a lot and you work so hard. I wanted to help."

"You went to the woods alone?" She pressed her forehead against his back, and her voice lowered to a tone that crushed me. "You went *alone*? How can I protect you when you do something like that? You . . ." Turning away from him, she stumbled toward the woods.

I went after her, remaining with her while she walked down a narrow trail weaving through the dense vegetation.

Finally, she stopped at the edge of the river, and I suspected she would've kept going if she hadn't reached the water.

She dropped to her knees and held her face in her hands.

I knelt with her and tugged her into my arms.

"You should stay with Brunnen," she said. "He's with those beasts."

"They won't hurt him. I want to be with you, Kaila. Protecting you. Holding you. Giving you whatever I can of myself to make you feel better." It hurt to swallow, to breathe.

"We're vulnerable out here. Why did I insist we leave the village? If we'd stayed, we would've been safe."

I didn't know what to say to that, so I said nothing, just held her while she trembled in my arms. She didn't cry, and I almost wished she would. That would release some of the tension thrumming through her body. It might give her peace.

"When I saw the shaydes surrounding him, I was terrified," she said, looking up at me. "I've done all I could to protect him, but they would've ripped him apart before I could get to him. They would've killed him and then . . . then I would've betrayed the promise I made to my parents after they died, that I'd keep him safe." Her gaze sadly took in the forest around us. "It's beautiful here. I'm sure there are other places just as lovely. But the forest is a beast coiled beneath the bushes, ready to strike." She shook her head. "I should've stayed in the village."

"Do you want me to take you back?" I'd do anything for her, even that.

"No." She eased out of my arms and stood. I remained where I was, kneeling before her, my heart held out in my hands. I didn't like the resolution I found shining in her eyes. "I know what I need to do." After stroking my face, she leaned into me, kissing me deeply. It caught my breath and swept me away. All I could think of was her and her exquisite touch.

She lifted her face and studied mine for a heartbeat before walking around me and back down the path.

Rising, I followed. I wanted to bellow, to charge through the woods. To sweep her up and take her to a place where she'd always feel secure. Protected. Loved.

But I wasn't sure that place existed.

We returned to the meadow to find Brunnen waiting, though the shaydes were gone.

"I was patting them when they suddenly turned around and bolted into the woods." He pointed toward where we would soon be heading. "I don't think I did anything to make them leave."

"Maybe they heard something and went to investigate," I said. I couldn't take my eyes off Kaila, watching her posture and her eyes that gave nothing away.

She studiously avoided looking at me.

I sensed the progress I'd made last night had been negated by the shaydes, but I didn't know what I could do about it. I was nearly out of time, and I hated that the fates would hold her out to me, then snatch her away.

"Are you ready to leave?" she asked both Brunnen and I.

We nodded and returned to where we'd left our things hooked to a low branch. After eating the food left from the night before, we started walking.

I wanted to keep our pace slow. Kaila appeared ready to run. And with each step, my heart grew heavier.

Mid-morning, sunlight slaked through the vegetation ahead when I spied the walls of the village.

"Almost there," I said. I wanted to ask Kaila—no, *beg* her—to stay with me, but I was beginning to suspect it was over. Like in my past, I'd done my best, and it wasn't good enough. The thought crushed me.

I wasn't giving up. As long as I could still suck in wind and lift my arms to hold them out to her, I wouldn't give up. But how could you convince someone to love you when they saw you as the one thing they feared above all others?

We stopped at the edge of the forest.

The guard on the wall saw us and lifted their spear. "Hello?"

"It's Turren," I called out. I'd visited the village

days before the mate hunt, when my heart was full of hope, and I was excited to think I might get to bond with a mate.

My hope was crumbling fast, and only a smile from Kaila would shore it up, a smile she wasn't sending my way. She stared toward the fortress with hunger, and I knew why. She saw it like it was her old village, only better. It would give her the security she craved, the stability she'd floundered to hold onto since her parents died.

I could give this to her, and I'd tried to show her, tell her, how wonderful it would be not just to stand by my side but to walk through the desert and mountain passes with me. I ached to share the beauty of my world with her, to show her how amazing that life could be.

But I'd never force her. If she came with me, it had to be because she not only trusted me, but because she believed that life with me would give her everything she needed.

"I've brought two humans to talk to the caedos about living within the walls," I added when Brunnen and Kaila remained silent and hidden among the forest shadows.

"Welcome, Turren," the guard said, lowering her spear. "Send them forward."

I looked their way.

Brunnen looked confused and sad. Kaila appeared determined, the resolution she'd come to in the forest still thriving within her. They stepped from the woods.

I remained behind. I couldn't do it. Going with them meant saying goodbye.

Did warriors cry?

"What are your names?" the leader of the village, Mavileen, shouted from the top of the wall.

Brunnen stopped. Kaila took a few steps farther before turning back to look his way. Her gaze drifted across me where I remained hidden, but I couldn't tell what she was thinking or feeling.

Actually, I knew. I just didn't want to admit it to myself.

"I'm Kaila," she said, turning back to Mavileen. She extended her hand to her brother. "This is my brother, Brunnen. We'd . . ." Her lungs expanded then released. "We've come seeking a place in your village. I worked in the gardens where we used to live, and my brother's quite eager to apprentice with a smithy. He helped the smithy in our old village."

"Both of you are welcome," Mavileen said, her gaze pinning me in place inside the forest. "Will you come with them, Turren?"

Should I? Would a few more hours make any difference, or would it just make it harder for me to tell her goodbye?

"No?" Mavileen said. "Know you're welcome at any time, my friend."

I saluted her and waited.

As the gate started to open, Kaila looked back at me. Only now could I read sorrow there, but it wasn't enough to change her mind.

I'd done my best. I'd truly tried. There wasn't anything more I could do.

My chest caved in, and a guttural cry rose up my throat. I bit it back as my pendant blazed, shouting out that she was mine. I was hers. We belonged together.

Just one more time, I wanted to lean close to her. Bury my face in her glorious hair and breathe in her scent, her warmth.

Turning, she faced the fortress once more. She extended her hand to Brunnen. He looked back at me and shook his head.

Then she tugged him forward, through the opening of the gate.

She walked away from me.

She took all I was with her.

CHAPTER 23

KAILA

I walked on dead feet, my heart a lump so big in my chest it was going to break through my ribs.

"What are you doing?" Brunnen hissed as the gate swung closed behind us.

"You know what I'm doing. Starting a new life for us. This place looks good."

I looked around the big open market area, taking in vendors selling their wares and women walking past leading farm animals. This village was big, almost half the size of our old one. Wooden homes had been built around the outside of the market, and beyond, I spied narrow roads lined with more buildings. I also picked up rows of greenery. A garden!

The village was full of women. I saw a few male orcs, but no human men.

"Welcome," a woman with dark skin said, striding

down stairs that led to the top of the wall. She walked over to join us, giving us both a smile. "I'm Mavileen."

"Kaila," I said weakly. Everything inside me told me this was wrong, that my place was with Turren even if that meant living in the mountains or a vast, dangerous desert.

Security, I reminded my stupid heart that continued to throb. *Keep Brunnen safe.*

Why did those words not bring me the comfort they had back in our old village?

"This is my brother, Brunnen," I said. "We're excited to be here."

Brunnen scowled and crossed his arms on his chest. "No, we're not."

"Brother," I scolded. "It's polite to greet someone when they welcome you into their village."

"We don't belong here," he said simply.

Mavileen's eyebrows lifted. "Do you two need a few moments alone to talk?"

"Yes, please." Heat flooded my face, chasing away my gut-wrenching sorrow if for only a few moments. "I'm sorry. Would you . . . ?"

She flashed a smile. "No worries. I'll wait over there." Her arm lifted to where a few women stood, bristling with weapons. "When you're ready, come to me. We have vacant homes for those who find their way to us, and I'll gladly take you to one and help you get settled. You can rest, and in a few days, we'll talk about where you fit in the village."

"Thank you." As she strode over to the others, I reeled around to face Brunnen. "What are you doing? We both decided to leave the village and come here. Now you're balking?" I wanted to cry. Not only because we'd put up with so much to get here but because . . .

All I could think of was Turren standing solemnly in the forest. Was he still looking this way, still hoping I'd change my mind, or had he turned and strode back into the woods, heading toward his beloved desert home?

I should be with him, a big voice inside me said, but I stomped her flat and glared at Brunnen.

"We don't belong here," he said again. "We might've when we left our village but not any longer. I can't believe you walked away from Turren, that you made me come with you."

"Are you saying you want to return to our old village?" I was floundering in emotions. They kept dropping down over me, smothering me.

And here he was, angry that we'd left the village we'd come from?

"I don't want to go back there," he said with disgust.

"Then you want to be here. Well, we're here." Fury rose inside me, a plague that would threaten everything I loved, even myself. I started stomping around in front of him, making dirt flick up from my heels. "I sacrificed a lot to come here. We were safe there."

"Other than your boss wanting you in his bed."

"I didn't choose to be with him."

"Do you really think he was giving you a choice? I saw the way he looked at you. You think I'm too young to understand anything but I'm not." His voice trembled but he kept going, raking away at the walls I was struggling to build around my heart. "He wanted you and he was going to take you. As for me, I would've been shoved out onto the street. He didn't care what happened to me."

"I wouldn't have allowed that to happen."

"You sound as if you think that even in this, you'd also have a choice. We had no choices in our old village." He peered around, squinting in the sunshine. "Here? It looks good. A nice place for anyone to settle. A *safe* place. Lots of guards, high walls, and they're friendly with the orcs. What could be better?"

"Then why are you complaining? We're here. We'll soon settle into our new home. I'll get a job and our life will be better."

"How can it be when your heart is breaking?"

I pressed my palm against my chest. "Don't say that. It's not true."

"It is. I saw how much Turren loves you."

"He's following the guidance of his fates. That's not love."

"How could you miss it? He did everything for us, gave up all he had just to impress you. And you're throwing him away as if he means nothing to you. But I see it." He poked my chest. "You love him too."

I did, but it couldn't matter.

I clutched the pendant he'd given me. It was precious and beautiful—like him. "He offers no stability. He and his clan move about from the desert to the mountains, barely knowing where they'll sleep the next night."

"That's not true. He explained how they live. They travel but they always have a destination, be it in the mountains on one side of the desert where the voxes mate and lay their eggs or in the low areas around an oasis. Don't you want to see that, live that?"

"It's full of uncertainty," I snarled. "Too many dangers. He told us about those as well."

"Because he wanted us to clearly see what we faced."

"It's too much. Too scary. I can't risk your life like that."

"You're afraid." He shook his head and for the first time since I'd taken over raising him, I saw disappointment on his face. It sliced through me like a blade, severing something vital inside me.

"I'm not afraid." For good measure, I poked him in the chest like he'd done to me.

"But you are." He held up his hand before I could sputter, let alone speak. "And I understand. Who wouldn't be afraid of taking a risk like that? We're used to fortress walls, plus the walls of a home around us. We're used to getting up and going to work, to collecting our pay and buying food. Sleeping and getting up to do it all over again. Day after day, always the same thing. Security? I suppose we had that, as long as you could keep working. Certainty? We had that as well, though I'll admit that to me, that life sounds boring. And the last one, the one word I know you treasure over almost anything. Stability. We even had that back in the old village."

"You don't understand." My voice shook. *I* shook. He was naming all the bits and parts of my soul that made up everything that was me.

"I do. Mom and Dad were killed. You've done an amazing job, being not just the best big sister I could ever ask for, but a parent. I'll be grateful to you for the rest of my life." He braced his hands on my upper arms, holding me still when all I wanted to do was run. I'd keep going forever. Keep going until I dropped.

And then, I suspected, I'd sob.

I was standing inside the village that had been our goal, and I still wasn't happy.

"You really . . . can't know how I'm feeling. Everything I've done was for you."

"Don't make this about me," he said, tipping my chin, making me meet his eyes. "This is all on you. You chose to toss aside someone you loved to make sure I'd continue to grow up in safety, but I won't take what you need from you."

"You're not taking anything." I cupped his dear

face. Gosh, he just kept growing taller. Our dad had been huge, almost as tall as an orc, and my brother was going to rival that height. "I'm giving you everything I have to make sure you grow up as you should. You're still a child. You have no say in this."

"Actually, I do." He stepped back, away from me, and whatever he took from me hurt. It left me in gut-wrenching, soul-crushing pain.

He lifted his spear that lay on the ground beside his feet and started walking toward the fortress gate.

"Where are you going?" I raced after him.

"This isn't the life I want."

"It's the only life you can have." Anger burst inside me, writhing like a serpent about to strike. "I've given up everything to raise you. At twelve, a year younger than you, I had to stop being a child and become a parent. I got a job, and I worked all the damn time. I kept our house clean, I cooked, and I sat with you when you were sick. I kept nothing for myself."

He turned back and he looked so sad, I wanted to hug him. He was my little brother and he needed me, but I suspected whatever I offered him now would never be enough.

"Then we'll stay. I'll continue to be your little brother while you work incredibly hard. I'm very proud of you, don't you know? I'll eat the meals you make and keep experimenting with cooking myself, because I think I'm pretty good at it."

"You are," I croaked.

"I'll get an apprenticeship with the smithy here, if they have one, or with someone. A carpenter or a mason. It doesn't really matter. It's a job. Security. Boring and without the sun setting across a vast open plain, but who needs something like that? I guess what we'll build here will someday be enough."

Pivoting, he started walking toward Mavileen, but he turned back. "You could change all this, change both our futures, and I bet you'd find it's so much better."

I wasn't sure what he meant. Actually, deep inside, I *did* know. I just didn't want to admit it.

"Can I?" I was a hollowed-out core. Nothing, if I couldn't cling to the purpose that had driven me for the past ten years.

"You can if you shove the fear away and let life give you the best gift in the world."

Again, I fell back to my overwhelming need for stability, for certainty. "I can't wander around the desert for the rest of my life."

"Not even if it means being with Turren?"

CHAPTER 24

TURREN

I stood inside the woods. How long would I remain here?

I sat. It would be a while before I got hungry. Before I needed to lay down somewhere and sleep.

Tiny flowers grew in profusion by my feet, pink things that looked so delicate that one stomp would crush them. I squatted and ran my fingertips across them, finding their stems sturdier than they looked. When I lifted my hand away, they sprung back up, looking as good as they had before I touched them.

They reminded me of Kaila. She was tiny and her skin was delicate and soft. She looked as if she could break easily yet she hadn't. At a young age, she'd stepped in and raised her little brother. She'd shown him love, and she'd given him everything he needed.

She was so much stronger than she knew. I should've told her that.

Now I'd never tell her anything.

I should turn away. My clan needed me. The new life I'd built with them was waiting.

I'd been gone too long already. They knew I'd hoped to find a mate during the hunt, and if I did, I'd bring her to them. Now I had a mate, but I'd return to my people without her.

My stupid pendant blazed. Would it ever give up? I wasn't sure *I* could, but I had to. I could remain here, waiting to court Kaila if she appeared on the wall or even go inside and walk through the village, but that was foolish. She'd made her choice, and it wasn't me.

A sound echoed from the fortress, but I didn't look up. I kept stroking the flowers, watching them flutter from my touch but spring back once more.

When a shadow fell over me, I still didn't look up. I assumed it was Mavileen, here to invite me to visit the village again. She'd welcomed me when I came with the others, and there was a place by her fire for me whenever I had need.

But entering the fortress meant seeing Kaila once more. I wanted that so much, but I knew that watching her begin a new life that didn't include me would kill me. When I left, I'd be nothing more than a shell with no Turren left inside. Everything I was would remain with her while I struggled to walk away.

"I was wondering," someone croaked.

I looked up and fell to my knees when I found Kaila standing there. Looking around her, I didn't see Brunnen, but right now, I didn't care. He must be inside the fortress.

Kaila was *here*.

"What are you wondering?" I asked.

She stroked her fingertips down my face. "The village offers stability."

"It does." I rose to my feet, looking down at her. She was so pretty, so delicate. Much too pretty or delicate for a scarred orc like me. I hadn't even told her the worst—or the best. I hadn't dared. Still didn't.

"The new village offers a certain future. They're offering me a home to live in, a job."

"That's wonderful," I rasped.

"It's wrapped up like someone has presented it to me as a gift with a big bow on top."

"It's what you need."

She frowned.

"I'm glad for you," I added. What else did she want me to say? Those words tasted bitter on my tongue, but all I'd ever want was for her to feel safe and happy.

"There's one big thing missing, though, and I thought you could help."

"What do you need? I'll give it to you. Anything."

"You. There's no Turren in the village."

Could I give up my life in the desert and mountains, of being the caedos of my people? It was so much more than that, though. That secret . . .

I would do this; find a way if she asked, but

nothing would hold value if she wasn't standing beside me.

"I could . . . live in the village." Mavileen would accept me there. "I'm strong. I work hard. And I'd do anything they asked of me."

I'd sacrifice everything that made me Turren as long as I could be with Kaila.

"See, there's one problem with that."

Why wasn't her frown going away? I'd just offered to live in the village, to make sure she had the stability and certainty that only a life behind fortress walls could offer.

"What's the problem?" I asked.

"The forest surrounds the village."

"Like the village you left." I didn't understand, but I was trying. Because her wants and needs were all that mattered.

"There's no vast sky above. The sun doesn't cut across that sky in the morning in pinks, golds, and orange. It doesn't paint the air. And in the evening, when the sun's setting, I won't see the red and orange so vivid my heart will want to soar up and grab onto those beams."

She was repeating the words I'd told her when I described the desert, but I still didn't know what she meant. What she needed.

"Tell me," I growled, though I wasn't mad. My heart was smacking against my ribs, telling me to let it out so it could surround Kaila and hold her close.

"I want to see the sand shifting, forming new peaks and being smoothed by the wind. I want to see the mountains, feel the snow on my face. I need to feel alive in a way I never have before."

"I'd give that to you if I could."

She held her hand toward me. "I don't want you to live in the village."

"I see." But I didn't. I couldn't see past the woods around us, the fortress walls, the tall grass that overwhelmed this part of the world.

"I want to live in the vast open spaces, to travel from an oasis to the vox nesting grounds. I want to stand by your side while you help your people. I want to lay my head next to yours at night and love you."

"Mate," I croaked, unable to believe what I was hearing but so overjoyed I couldn't think. All I could do was *feel*.

Her tentative smile rose, and she nodded. "Mate."

I brushed her hand aside but held out my arms.

And she leaped into them.

CHAPTER 25
KAILA

I was hugging him, kissing him, and my heart was overflowing.

"I love you. I want to be with you always," I said.

"My precious mate. My beloved mate." He peppered my face with kisses. "I adore you. I love you, and I will until my dying day and beyond."

"I'd be wrong to say I'm not nervous about this, but no matter what, my feelings for you matter most."

"I promise, you won't regret this. Never."

"Does this mean we're going to live with the Ember Clan?" Brunnen dropped our bags on the ground nearby.

Turren grinned at me. "What do you say, mate? Are we going to the mountains where my clan has recently settled for the summer?"

Tension coiled tight inside me, and an ongoing

battle was being waged, but being with Turren was winning the fight.

"We are." I said it with enough conviction, Turren laughed.

He spun me around and kissed me again. I speared my fingers into his hair, clinging to this male I adored very much. Everything felt right when I was in his arms. Life was perfect, the way it was supposed to be.

"Are we going to stand here all day while you two kiss?" Brunnen's words broke through the passion spiraling between us.

I burst away from Turren, laughing. "Don't you like kisses, brother?"

He sighed. "I'm thirteen, not twenty. Frankly, I can't see why anyone wants to put their mouth on someone else's." He lifted the bags. "More walking, I assume."

"Not so." Turren gently released me, and I slid down his body. His pendant blazed.

Claiming was in our future, both for him and for me, and I couldn't wait.

"Let's go tell Mavileen that you're both coming with me and . . ." He took my hand and kissed it, sending tingles flashing through my body. "And I'll show you a much faster way to reach my mountain home."

He held my hand as we approached the fortress, and this time, they opened the gate before we got there. We went inside and Mavileen greeted us with her women warriors flanking her, holding various weapons. I'd never seen anything like it. They wore simple clothing and not much of it. No long skirts to hamper movement or full blouses that got in the way. Each wore bands of leather around their breasts, with their tautly muscled bellies showing, and loincloths like what Turren wore, only scooped underneath and wrapped around their hips in addition to flaps on the front and back for modesty.

What would it be like to wear such an outfit? My body heated because I knew what Turren would think if he saw me dressed in such a way.

"Welcome," Mavileen said with a smile, her gaze shooting to our clasped hands. "Can I assume you're no longer seeking sanctuary in our village, Kaila?"

I shook my head. "I'm sorry. Your offer is generous." My eyes stung with tears. These women had welcomed me easily when my own fellow villagers had made me feel eager to run. "I love Turren, and I'm going to live with him and the Ember Clan." My new people. What would they think of their caedos mating with a human?

I would soon find out.

"I well understand," she said.

Turren's pendant flared, and she shielded her eyes. "Not fully mated yet, I see?"

Heat climbed into my face. "We've been . . ."

Turren's fingers tightened around mine. "Finding our way to each other."

He sounded relaxed about this. We were talking about having sex! But when an orc came up behind Mavileen and wrapped his arms around her and kissed her neck, I understood. His pendant didn't flare, and it was only now that I noticed she was carrying a child—his, I assumed.

If Turren and I had sex, which I suspected we would soon do, would I one day carry our child? A fierce longing filled me, and I knew that yes, so much yes, I wanted that.

"I see," Mavileen said. "Will you be staying for long? Know you're welcome here for as long as you wish to remain."

"I'd like to buy some provisions," Turren said. "But I'll call my vox, and he'll take us to the mountain home of my clan."

"It's almost time for the voxes to return to the hills for breeding, isn't it?" she asked, leaning into the orc's embrace. Catching my eye, she smiled and nodded as if to say, see, orcs are amazing, aren't they? "This is my mate, Pulost."

"Welcome," he murmured, easing around Mavileen to stand beside her with his arm around her shoulders.

"As for buying provisions, it would be an honor to help you with this. We'll give you a bargain," Mavileen said with a low laugh. She turned. "Call your vox, and we can walk through the market together."

"Will I ride on the vox as well?" Brunnen asked.

"Three is too much for Airest, but we'll find another way to get you there," Turren said.

"If you'd like, I can ask the Matis Clan if one of the shaydes could take him to the edge of the desert," Pulost said. "They've helped in this way before."

Brunnen sucked in a breath. "You mean I'd *ride* on a shayde?"

"We met them in the forest," I said. "They're . . ." Alright, I was going to look at all this differently. If I didn't, I'd cling to fear forever, something I didn't want to do. "They're amazing."

Turren shot me a smile and squeezed my hand. "They truly are."

"Yes, you'd ride on a shayde," Pulost said with a grin sent my brother's way.

"Wow," Brunnen breathed. "I can't wait."

We strolled through the market, Turren buying dried fruit and nut cakes and a few more flasks to carry water.

"How long will it take to get to our home?" I asked. It was daring of me to call it that, but if my place was with Turren, it was my home too.

"We'll fly at night and rest during the day when the shaydes aren't hunting. Once we reach my clan, I'll send someone to collect Brunnen on the edge of the desert."

We'd be alone during that time. My heart flipped over at the thought. I felt as if I knew him very well. My heart knew him completely. Yet we'd only been together a few days. I wanted to be alone with him, to speak with him about anything and everything, to *touch* him.

"A shayde?" Brunnen kept saying, his eyes wide with wonder. "Will someone ride with me or . . ."

"We tell them what we need, though I doubt you'll ride alone," Pulost said in an indulgent tone. "Someone will go with you. The shaydes can hold two." He rubbed Brunnen's shoulder and took him over to a smithy shop where a woman stood behind a table with wares for sale. "See anything you like? A male of the Ember Clan needs a good blade."

Brunnen gulped.

I walked over quickly, trying not to cringe. "They're all amazing, and I agree with you, Pulost, but . . . we can't afford anything like that." Maybe once I'd settled with the Ember Clan, I could start a garden and grow vegetables to sell. Then I could take my brother to a market where he could select a blade.

"This would be a gift from our village to Brunnen, if that is acceptable to you." I could tell by the soft look in Pulost's eyes he knew exactly what I was speaking of.

This made me even more embarrassed, though I shouldn't be. I'd worked hard to get us to this point in our lives, and I was proud of what I'd been able provide my brother, not ashamed of what I couldn't.

"Varalar owes me, don't you?" Pulost said with humor.

The woman, Varalar, huffed. "I owe him a lot." Her intent gaze met mine. "You don't know how it is at some villages. Women . . ."

"I suspect I do. We're considered . . . lesser."

"Exactly." She shook her head. "My father was going to give me to a man. Give me! Not marry me to him, oh, no, but outright hand me to him just because he wanted to impress the man. After all those years working beside him at his smithy, he still couldn't see my value as a person. That night, I took my things and ran into the woods. If members of the Matis Clan hadn't found me and brought me here," a shudder tracked through her body, "well, I know what would've happened." Her gaze shot in the direction of the forest. "And It would've been a better ending than the one my father planned for me. That man . . . I not only didn't love him, but he was also cruel."

"We fled our village as well," Brunnen said. "For a similar reason, though not guided by our parents." He took my other hand and squeezed it. "I'm going to be a better man than Jabon, a better man that Varalar's father."

"I know you are." My brother was soft where he needed to be and strong where it fit best. I'd done a good job raising him, and I wasn't afraid to admit it.

"Then you do understand," Varalar said. "I arrived here with nothing but some clothing. No tools, no food, no coins. And you know what the people here did? They gave me a home. They helped me build a smithy. And Pulost traveled to the orc city where he bought tools and brought them here, gifting them to me. It was incredible and I'll never find a way to fully repay him."

"You needed them," he said, his face darkening. "It was nothing."

Leaning forward, she nudged his arm. "It was *everything*, and you well know it." Her smile rose when she looked back at me. "So, when I say that a friend of Pulost is a friend of mine and that your brother can choose whatever weapon he wants for free, I mean it. It would be an honor to arm such a young man."

I was going to cry. No, I *was* crying.

"Mate," Turren said, his frantic gaze scanning the area as if he thought there was a threat. "What is it? Tell me." He turned me and cupped my face, tilting it to examine me. "Are you injured? Please. Tell me what I can do to see the light of happiness come back into your eyes."

"I'm happy." I grinned through my tears. "Very happy. Women sometimes cry when we're feeling joy, not only when we're sad."

"That's the truth," Varalar said. "You should've seen me when Pulost presented me with a cart load of tools. I dropped to my knees and sobbed."

Pulost nodded solemnly. "I thought I'd somehow wounded her when I'd only been trying to help."

"My mate is incredible." Even Mavileen had tears in her eyes now. "To think I rejected him at first."

"You fell in love with me immediately," he said sternly, though with a sparkle in his dark eyes. "I only had to convince you of that fact." He looked our way. "The fates of my clan chose her, but even if my pendant hadn't flamed, I would've known right away that she was the only woman I'd ever love."

"You." She stroked his jawline, and he kissed her palm, kissing her lips after. "I did take a bit of persuading, but I'm grateful I gave us a chance." She looked my way. "Please. I know what it's like to feel uncomfortable accepting gifts. Many of us here started with nothing. We've all worked hard to get to where we are today, which is thriving. Happy. But know that what we give you today is a gift from our hearts. I do hope you'll take it."

"Very well," I said, wiping the tears from my eyes.

Brunnen jerked out a nod, clearly nervous about all this. He, like me, wasn't comfortable with someone giving us things. In the past, nothing had ever been given without the expectation of a return favor—often something we'd never otherwise offer them.

"Whichever appeals," Pulost said. He went on to describe the blades for sale, pointing to those he felt had the best grip and those he believed would not only suit my brother now but work well for him when he was fully grown.

Finally, Brunnen settled on one. He tilted it this way and that, the sunlight winking off the sharp edge, and I couldn't stop smiling. "It's amazing," he gushed to both Pulost and Varalar. "I can't thank you enough."

"You'll need a sheath, or you'll risk wounding yourself," she said in a practical manner, handing a leather belt with a sheath to him as well.

He reverently laid the blade on the table and quickly donned the belt, noting that the waistband had room to expand as he grew bigger and taller. Then he slid the blade into the sheath and stepped back, his gaze sweeping across all of us. "What do you think? Does it look alright?'

"It looks good on you," I said, my eyes stinging once more.

Truly, this had been an incredible, wonderful day.

CHAPTER 26
TURREN

After collecting supplies, the villagers refusing to accept payment—though they agreed I could come back soon to bring rare items from the desert and mountains—we went to Mavileen and Pulost's home and ate.

By then, it was starting to get dark.

Because Airest wouldn't arrive until the next day, we opted to stay with Mavileen and Pulost, though we shared a room with Brunnen.

I held my mate through the night, giving her chaste kisses after Brunnen finally fell asleep. I couldn't wait until we were alone, which we would be while we traveled.

The next morning, Mavileen took us on a tour of the village. It was incredible to see all the progress they'd made in such a short time. When Dakur and I visited before the hunt, we'd only stopped briefly for introductions.

"And that's it," Mavileen said, her arm sweeping out toward the gardens. "We'll have an amazing harvest and will be able to store a lot of food for the cold months. We hunt with the Matis Clan, sharing the kills, and I'll honestly admit that they're much better at that than most of us women. Some of us were *allowed*," she scowled, "to do simple trapping or set snares, but most of us aren't proficient yet with a bow or other weapons. The orcs are training us."

Pulost's chest puffed with pride. "That's my contribution to the village."

"Among others," she said with a smile. "I'm caedos here, but that's a new role for me as well. Pulost knows a lot about how to run a clan, and I'm incorporating a lot of his ideas into what we do in the village. We're a blend of both worlds now that many of the women have found orc mates. I think the combination only makes us all better."

We were having lunch with them when a few Matis Clan members arrived outside the fortress walls. They entered the compound, and I strode over to them.

"Dakur." I braced his forearms. "It's good to see you again." I nodded to his new mate, Nia. Nia had lived with her stepbrother in a village deep within the desert, near an oasis. Her stepbrother had been a cruel person, and he'd purchased Dakur to use him in a fighting arena with the intent of making him battle until he met a match he couldn't defeat. Nia and Dakur fell in love and escaped the compound where Dakur was being held in chains. They'd made it part way across the desert, and we saw them while flying overhead on our voxes. They'd stayed with my clan for a time after that, and then we flew them to their Matis Clan home.

"So nice to see you." Nia gave me a hug before returning to the shelter of Dakur's arms. She reached above her shoulder, and he took her hand, kissing it before resting it on her shoulder. They were happy together.

It used to make my heart hurt. Now I had Kaila. My own love. The envy had left my heart, replaced with pure joy.

I introduced them to my mate. My pendant blazed —again. The damn thing had been lighting off almost constantly. I understood why. I was supposed to claim her before someone else's pendant did the same and they challenged me for the honor of becoming her full mate. That had happened to another orc, and he had to compete in a series of tests in order to solidify his claim to the woman he loved. Madr and his mate, Lyneth, lived in the orc city, and I'd met them recently. They were also incredibly happy.

A few other orcs came with Dakur—and a shayde.

The shayde loped forward and leaped toward me. I'd already been a part of that, thank you. Scooping up Kaila, I stepped to the side.

Brunnen laughed and rushed forward, tackling the shayde—mostly. He barreled into the beast who leaned a bit from the blow but didn't fall. Soon the two were racing around, playing, with Brunnen's laughter echoing around us.

"I still shudder when I see them," Mavileen said. "I can't tell if they're one of the Matis Clan shaydes or one I have to run from." She lifted her spear. "I keep this handy at all times."

"You'll eventually recognize them," Dakur said. "They have distinctive personalities and coloring."

"As you say." Mavileen didn't sound convinced of that.

"Taen will take Kaila's brother to the edge of the desert," Dakur told me. "He'll meet up with whoever you send to collect him there. Taen can't travel as fast through the forest as your vox will fly above, however, so plan to send someone once you reach the mountains."

"He's not traveling alone on a shayde, is he?" Kaila said with a touch of fear in her voice.

"While he could, I'm not sure that would be best. Your brother's strong, and I know he'd do well on his own, but why risk him?" Dakur said. "One of my clansmen will travel with him and return on Taen."

A smaller orc stepped from the woods, and I guessed he was a few years older than Brunnen.

"Reven is looking forward to the adventure," Dakur said, putting his arm around Reven's shoulders. "He's seventeen and very good at not only defending himself and others, but hunting. He'll make sure Brunnen reaches the desert safely and will wait with him until someone arrives on a vox."

Kaila nodded, giving me a quick smile, and I was grateful to Dakur for thinking of bringing a traveling companion. Reven and Brunnen would get along well, and Brunnen could continue his training with his staff when they stopped to rest at the end of the day.

"We've gathered our things," I said. "We're just waiting for . . ."

I heard the wing beats before I saw him.

Kaila gasped as my vox flew overhead, calling out when he saw me. He circled the village and landed on a hill off to the side in the open area between the fortress and the forest.

"There he is," I said. "We'll make sure he eats and has plenty of water, plus enough rest, and then we'll start our journey." I squeezed Kaila's hand. "Are you ready to travel on a vox?"

"It's enormous," she said in breathy jerks. "Incredibly big." She grinned my way again. "But yes, my mate, I'm looking forward to our journey." From the heat in her eyes, I suspected she was looking forward to the times when we'd stop more than the travel itself, but she'd soon be savoring the wonder of flight just like I did.

"Would you like to meet him?" I asked.

She sucked in a breath, and her eyes widened. "Yes, I actually would."

We left the others, Brunnen still playing with Taen like he was a shayde kit, and walked up the hill to where Airest waited. I took Kaila to Airest's head.

"Airest? This is my mate, Kaila," I said solemnly. "My strong, adventurous mate. The woman I adore, and who I'll love forever."

"I still can't believe we're together," she said, though with a happy sigh.

"Always."

"Should I bow or . . . I don't know voxes at all. How should I greet him?" Her voice came out a bit shrill, but that was understandable. Until a short time ago, she'd never heard of, let alone seen a vox. At first sight, they could be intimidating.

"Airest would love to sniff your hand, and have you stroke his face," I said. "He loves having his ears scratched in particular."

"Truly?"

"Truly."

I showed her what I meant, rubbing the side of Airest's face while he purred. When I reached his ears, he stretched out his neck and groaned, his eyes closing while I rubbed. "I believe my brave mate will enjoy it when I rub her like this."

"Do you plan to rub her ears?" Kaila asked with a snort.

"I intend to nibble on her ears, her neck, plus many other areas as soon as we're alone."

"I can't wait for that," she said in a dreamy voice.

When Airest nudged her belly, she sucked in a breath before tentatively touching the vox's face. Airest continued to purr, and my mate became the bold female I'd named her. She walked to the side of Airest's head and started scratching the vox's ears to Airest's delight.

"He's amazing," she said in awe. "I'm stunned. Will I bond with my own vox one day?"

"If you wish."

"I want to. I don't know what to do with one or how to train it, but I sense this would be a highlight in my life."

"Most of my clan have bonded with voxes. There are many who travel with us. Sometimes, we walk to our next destination, but more often than not, we load our things on voxes and fly."

"Then it probably doesn't take long to go from one destination to another."

I shook my head. "Sometimes only a day or two. We enjoy stopping. When we're out in the open like that, there's less light, and the stars . . . Well, you'll have to see them to believe it yourself. I've tried to find the right words to describe the feeling in my heart, to share my words, but the best way is to show you."

Which I would very soon. I couldn't wait to show off every bit of my life with Kaila.

"You've mentioned not being comfortable speaking before."

"I learned to be quiet when I was young. It was hard at first, but I soon saw that when I didn't speak, things . . . went better. But I need to find my words and give them voice, especially with you, Kaira."

"You have." She came over to lean against me. "I love hearing words from your heart."

Then I'd find the way to say them often.

"I assume Airest is tired. I'll help you bring him food and water."

"He'll drink from the river. Fish, too, because he loves them, but I'll bring out a few haunches of meat for him later."

"How long will he need to rest?"

"A few hours. We should be ready to leave at dusk."

"I'm ready now." Returning to stand in front of me, she wrapped her arms around my body as far as she could reach. "Soon, we'll be alone. In the village, when a couple married, they would have time alone in their home before others started visiting. They called it a honeymoon."

"We'll have our honeymoon while traveling," I said. "But know that it won't stop there. I intend to show you that you made the right choice in joining with me. I'll make sure you never have regrets."

"I love you," she said simply. "You love me. And that's all that matters."

Would she still love me when she discovered what I was holding back?

Soon, I'd have to tell her.

There would be no hiding this from her for long.

CHAPTER 27

KAILA

I wrung my hands and fretted.

"Listen to Reven," I told my brother, gripping his fingers tight. "Do as he says. Don't act too silly. And make sure you're up in a tree before it gets dark."

He'd remain here with Reven, and they'd leave first thing in the morning. Like when we walked, the shayde would travel all day and rest at night—and hunt, I was sure. Meanwhile, my brother and Reven would eat, bathe and drink in the river, and climb trees before it got dark, remaining there until morning.

Reven seemed mature enough for this journey, but by the fates, he was young himself. Maybe this wasn't a good idea. I could—

"Mate." Turren tugged me back away from my brother. "He'll be fine. You'll see him in a few days."

"Yes, Kaila. Please." Brunnen looked around at our friends who'd come to see us off on the vox. "This is going to be an amazing adventure for me."

And that was the problem. I didn't want him going on an adventure. He was only thirteen. He might . . .

I realized where my mind was going, that I was spiraling back into the person I was before I decided to let the fates help decide, to trust that our orc friends would not only keep us safe but also give us a life we'd relish.

"I love you," Brunnen said, bursting into laughter before his voice lifted in pitch, mimicking me in a teasing way, only directing it toward my upcoming adventure. "Listen to Turren. Do as he says. Don't act silly. Kiss him if you must, but please, please, please, don't tell *me* too much about whatever other adventures you two get involved in."

I sighed and sniffed, refusing to cry. "I love you too."

He hugged me, speaking into my hair. "You've been the best sister a boy could ever have, but I'm growing up. Soon, I'll be a man, and I'll have my own life, *live* my own life." He stepped back. "Maybe I'll even find an orc female and kiss her." When he winked, I knew he was only joking. He might wind up with an orc *male*. I'd noted him looking at both males and females back at the village.

I'd love him no matter who he loved in turn.

"Be safe." He braced my shoulders, speaking to me like I was the child and he the substitute parent. "I'll see you in a short time."

Biting down hard on my lower lip, I nodded. I wasn't going to cry.

"Time to go, my courageous mate," Turren said in a low rumble.

I nodded and hugged Brunnen once more. Then I ran around hugging everyone who'd come to see us off. Dakur, Nia, Mavileen, and Pulost. Even Varalar had trekked up the hill to say goodbye.

"Alright, how do we do this?" I asked, striding over to Airest. The vox sniffed my hand delicately and nudged my chest in affection. He was huge, a giant dark green beast towering over me. And I was supposed to nonchalantly climb up onto his back and he'd . . . fly?

My knees shook, and my air came in short pants. My head was starting to spin, and I was beginning to believe I'd prefer to walk all the way to the mountains, even if they were on the other side of the desert.

Turren swept me up in his arms and with a quick leap, he landed on Airest's spine, his legs straddling the beast's back.

"Your inner thighs aren't used to riding," he said gently as he lowered me onto his lap, spreading my legs to go around him while I clung to his chest. "You'll have to change positions often, and we'll rest as much as we can." He lowered his head to speak for my ears alone. "And, when we stop, I'll be happy to rub ointment on your thighs and massage you wherever you're sore."

My spine tingled, and my breathing grew heavier. When I looked up at him, I marveled anew that he wanted me, that he loved me. He was the sweetest male I'd ever met, and I couldn't imagine why all the orc females hadn't tried to claim him.

"Does this massaging go both ways?" I asked coyly. "Because your thighs might get sore as well."

He barked out a laugh. "The days of me being sore from riding a vox have long since passed, but you're welcome to . . . massage me whenever you please, my precocious mate."

I pouted. "I think I like being your courageous mate more than your precocious mate."

He laughed again. "You're my *everything* mate."

Others handed up our belongings in packs, and Turren hooked the straps onto the spike jutting up from Airest's spine where it met his neck.

"Goodbye," Brunnen called out. "Have fun!"

Fun. Yes. This was supposed to be fun?

The beast shifted beneath us, and I wondered how we wouldn't just . . . fall off and tumble through the sky. Smack on the ground or into the trees.

My heart started pattering again, and my belly kept surging up my throat. I swallowed it down along with my fear as best I could.

And if I clung Turren . . . Alright, if I shrieked and wrapped myself around him when Airest burst up into the sky, well . . . that only proved his point. I was a bit of everything. But for now, I was going to try my best to be his courageous mate.

Flying wasn't as terrifying as I thought it would be. Yes, it was a bit scary being so far off the ground, but the world opened up for me, expanding to include a lush forest below, mountains far in the distance, and a dark sky overhead ripe with stars and a half moon.

I stopped clinging to Turren and relaxed, enjoying the soothing flap of Airest's wings and the way my mate's heart thudded beneath my ear.

We talked, sharing everything about each other. Our first conversations had been a battle of wits, but now it was nice to hear why he loved being the caedos of his clan and to share some good stories from my own childhood before my parents died.

Sometime during the night, I fell asleep in his arms to the soothing sweep of Airest's wings. I woke when the vox landed and looked around, finding he'd settled in a small meadow with woods all around.

"Wake, my sleepy mate," Turren said softly in my ear.

I stretched, leaning into his embrace. "I'm awake, my loving mate."

His arms tightened around me. "Yes, I do love you."

I turned to face him, linking my legs around him, and his pendant blazed.

"I believe it's time for that to stop shining, don't you?" I shielded my face and winced as if it irritated me.

"Yes, well . . ."

Ha. He wasn't going to name it? I had no problem with that.

"I'm going to claim you, my lusty mate, and that'll put a stop to it," I boldly said.

His jaw dropped. What? He didn't think I planned to climb all over him the moment I got a chance? We were finally alone. I loved my brother, but I wouldn't want to be with Turren when my brother might overhear.

"Claim me?" He gulped.

I traced my fingertips across his jaw and down his chest. "Unless you'd like to wait."

"No," he croaked. "I'm done waiting." As if he shed a skin, he shrugged off the surprised and uncertain orc and the bold, sexy one I adored took his place.

His arms tightened around me, holding me close as he leaped off his vox. He landed squarely on the ground and peered around, looking for threats.

"I need to take care of Airest but then, my luscious mate, you're mine," he growled.

I helped him rub down the vox while it purred and crooned, clearly loving the attention.

"Will he wait here while we . . ." I had no idea why I was suddenly shy. I wanted to be with him more than anything. It was a chance to deepen our love, to show each other with touches and sighs how much we meant to each other.

"He'll go find something to eat," Turren said, coming around Airest to take my hand. "I've got a surprise for you, something Pulost mentioned."

"What is it?"

He took our bags from the ground where he'd placed them after taking them off his vox. "Let me show you. I think it'll have more meaning then."

Holding hands, we walked through the woods toward the river, eating fruit and nut bars from the village on the way. We sat on the bank and finished our meal, drinking water after.

"Let's swim," he said, rising.

"Is that the surprise? Because I'm not sure Pulost would bother to mention something like that." The tease came through in my voice.

He grinned. "No, the surprise will come after that. Wash quickly, my tempting mate, and then I'll show you."

While I'd love to stroke him in the water, my curiosity had been sparked. I cleansed my teeth and took a quick dip in the river, drying after. Before I could dress, however, Turren came up behind me, wrapping his wet body around mine.

"No clothing, my delectable mate."

I looked around. "It's a lovely river."

His laugh snorted out. "And you still believe this is the special place Pulost mentioned?"

I shrugged. "It is special."

"Nowhere special enough for you." His voice hollowed out. "I'm not sure such a place exists."

I turned in his arms and stroked his chest, loving how my hands slipped due to the wetness. His cock thrust between us, big and vigorous and gorgeous.

"Do women ever lick a male's cock?" I asked, my face coloring. Would he laugh?

"On occasion."

My breath caught and all the possibilities swam through my mind, making my pulse roar and heat flow from my belly to between my legs. "I want to try it."

"I will never tell you no, my audacious mate. Let me take you to the special place and then . . ." He took my hand and started walking along a trail beside the river.

"We're going for a stroll naked?" The bottoms of my feet protested each rock and stick I stepped on, slowing my pace to a crawl.

"You're too delicate for this." He swept me up into his arms and continued striding.

"I suspect being too delicate is not a good thing."

"It's wonderful. Knowing you need me makes me feel strong and brave."

"You're both." My voice cracked. "To me, you're everything. I don't believe I can find the words to tell you how much I adore you."

"They're in my heart, love. Every word, every feeling. There are no words that can describe how much I adore *you*, but I'll spend every day of my life trying to find them. And then I'll lay them in your delicate hands." Pausing, he kissed me, his lips soft and light on my mouth. I loved how he could take charge of everything, how he sometimes made demands. But when he was sweet like this, my heart cracked wide open. Could I love him more than I did right now?

He lifted his head and strode along the path. "Pulost said he found this place a few years ago. He doesn't believe anyone else knows of it. He hopes to bring Mavileen here one day, perhaps once the village is settled, and she has time to get away for a day or so."

"It's amazing that a woman is a mayor of a village, though since only women formed it, it makes sense. Women don't really need men."

"Not even for kisses?"

"That's sexual. We'll always need you for that. Even to have children."

He sucked in a breath and watched my face as he picked his way along the path. "Do you want children?"

"I haven't thought much about it. I think so. Maybe. I've already raised a child in my brother. What about you?"

"I . . ." His gaze lifted from mine to the path, and it appeared rocky, needing his attention, but I still sensed there was something going on within him, something he hadn't yet shared. "I adore orclings."

"I take herbs I purchased from a woman in the village. I brought some with me. They keep me from having children." I needed to spell that out for him. He shouldn't get his hopes up that being together could result in a child.

"You've been with males."

I didn't sense any recrimination in his words. "Only two. I . . . it was alright. I can't say it was wonderful."

He snorted. "I'm a bold male."

"You don't say."

"You'll find endless pleasure in my arms."

I suspected I would. "And yes, there's that bold Turren once more."

"I've only been with one person before. After my parents died, I was incredibly busy. I took over the role of caedos."

"Surely even a caedos takes time to relax, to be with someone in that way." I wasn't jealous he'd been with another. Why would I be? What he did before we met was history.

"I met her when I traveled to the Ballelt Clan. Neither of us wanted to be together again after that."

"Has she found her mate?" Alright, so perhaps I *could* feel a touch of jealousy.

"Not yet. It's rare for the fates to show us our true

mate, the one person we'll adore until our dying day. Many wait for that, never being with another."

It . . . might be awkward, but if we visited that clan, perhaps we'd be friends. My swallow went down hard, and unease settled into my bones. Tried to, that is. Turren and I were going to be together no matter what, and I wasn't going to let something like this stand between us.

He kept walking and with each step, my unease fled. How could I be worried about anything when I loved him?

"We're almost there," he said.

"How are your toes doing?"

He frowned. "My toes?"

"You're walking barefoot and there are rocks and sticks all over the path."

He looked down. "I didn't notice."

"You're tough in so many ways."

The boyish smile he gave me made my heart stumble. It picked itself up and raced after that.

"Yes, I'm tough."

I laughed, feeling carefree. "When are you going to put me down?"

"Close your eyes."

"Ah, so it's that kind of surprise?"

"Yes, that kind of surprise," he said.

I closed my eyes, and he kept walking, finally coming to a stop.

"You can open them now," he said softly.

I gasped. "This . . . is amazing. Are you sure the fates didn't collect us and take us to another world? I can't believe this place is hidden away in the forest."

I blinked, letting the flood of colors wash over me. The meadow stretched out like a painting, though I'd only seen a few of those in my life. Flowers of every color swayed in the breeze in hues so bright, it was like they'd been plucked from a rainbow.

"Do you like it?" Turren stroked my spine, his deep voice rumbling through the quiet air. "It's a garden. A beautiful garden just for you."

I leaned into his side, my heart bursting with love. "You remembered."

"I remember everything," he rasped. "You like it?"

"I love it. How did it end up here?"

"Pulost doesn't know. He believes someone planted the flowers long ago and they've thrived even without attention. Or nature did this for us. The fates work many wonders. I thought you'd like it since you enjoy gardening so much."

My eyes stung. "It's amazing. I don't want to step on even one flower."

He swept me up in his arms again. "Do you mind if I take you to the center? Pulost mentioned there's a smooth carpet of green there. No flowers to crush."

"Take me there, please," I breathed, eager to see it all.

Turren was a large orc, at least a hand's width taller than the orcs I'd met in the human village. And broader too. Yet he took delicate care as he walked through the meadow, gently brushing the flower stems to the side and placing his feet in a way that didn't squish them.

As he moved, the magic of this place sunk into me. It was hard to imagine life like this pulsing so brilliantly within the depths of an orc forest. They were a race known more for their strength and ferocity than delicate beauty.

"Did Pulost give this place a name?" I asked.

He shook his head. "We can call it whatever we please, something that has meaning to only us."

"Heart's beginning?"

He kissed me. "I like that. This is the beginning for us, love."

Walking a bit more, he arrived at the middle of the meadow, and I took in the perfect circle of purple vegetation with waxy leaves glistening in the light.

"It's beautiful."

"It's also soft on my feet," he said with a laugh. "You'll like it. No sore toes or crushing the flowers. This vegetation is springy, see?" He lifted his foot and the plants sprung back up to fill in the space where his foot had been.

I suspected us lying on it might change it a bit, but I wasn't as worried about making a mark on this perfect spot that should quickly return to the way it was before we got here.

"Put me down. I want to feel."

He slowly released me, and I slid down his front, noting his erection hadn't changed. I was going to taste it soon, but for now, it was time to feel it sinking deeply inside me.

"You're so tiny. So fragile and delicate," he said softly, holding my upper arms. "I don't want to ever cause you pain."

I shrugged. "Others have found a way to be together and we will too."

"Mate," he growled. He curled his body forward and tentatively placed his lips on mine.

I could kiss him forever. His lips were plump and full and so gentle. While his hands roamed my arms and back, he deepened the kiss.

I gasped, my mouth opening, and his tongue plundered, finding mine and stroking in a way that made everything inside me melt.

It was just him and I in this glorious place, the perfect spot for us to be together for the first time. Heart's beginning. I'd call that forever.

And I'd give up the world to be with him now.

Pure feelings shot through me, feeding my need for him, making me tremble.

He lifted me, and I wrapped my legs around him, pushing forward to feel his hard chest rub my thighs and that spot between them.

He held my bottom, squeezing and releasing, while his other hand stroked across my jaw. It amazed me that this big, burly orc could be so gentle, that he could put all his feelings into each stroke of his fingers across my skin.

My heart pounded, racing so fast, I thought it would stop. I stroked his chest, unable to get enough of his endless smooth skin. His fingers caressed my cheeks and moved down my neck, sliding around to my back to press my body against his. My nipples pebbled as I rubbed them against him.

I smoothed my hands along his left arm, carefully touching his scars, and he froze, lifting his head, watching me.

"You're beautiful," I said.

"Males are never beautiful. We're too full of hard edges and muscles."

"You are. *All* of you."

"I want to be beautiful if only in your eyes."

I smiled. "You always will be."

With his smoldering gaze locked on mine, he lowered me to the lavender carpet, following me down, his arms bracing on either side of me, his knee sliding up between my thighs.

I spread my legs and he groaned, kissing down my neck to my breasts.

His mouth was hot and insistent, sucking at my nipple, making it harden even further. He stroked the other, plucking at it, making me moan and writhe beneath him.

"Turren," I cried out. "I need . . ."

"I'm here for you, mate. Always," he murmured

against my flesh. "You're the brightest star in the sky, the deepest, clearest pool in the desert. And the sparkle of the rarest jewel deep within the caves of our mountains."

He said the sweetest things. I wanted to grab onto them and hold them inside my heart forever.

His mouth left my breast, and he kissed across my belly. When he parted my legs and crawled beneath them, he looked up at me with so much love, so much lust, it made my heart break.

Nothing and no one would ever compare to this moment, to this time when Turren and I would first come together. I'd always treasure that he'd wanted this to be perfect for us, that he'd brought me to this special place solely because he knew how much it would mean to me. Flowers and pretty vegetation didn't mean much to my love. He was a caedos, a male absorbed in the duties of his clan. Yet he was making sure I'd have a moment to cherish.

He slid his fingers across my slit, and his growl rang out. "So wet for me. Tell me what you like, how to drive you wild."

"Touch me. Put your fingers inside me."

He glided them through my folds and up to my clit, then back down again. Each time, he pushed his fingers deep inside me, almost pulsing them with me, only to tug them back out and stroke them across my clit.

I was a ball of fire shooting all the way to the sky. I

couldn't hold out for long, though I wanted to more than anything.

He plunged his fingers deeply, swirling them, curling them to stretch me.

And when I burst into flames, he caught me, holding me while bringing me back down to the gorgeous world around me.

CHAPTER 28
TURREN

"It's been too long since I tasted you, my glorious mate," I said as I spread her legs wider. She'd come for me, her cry of pleasure echoing in the meadow. But I wanted to take more. I'd suck on her until she came again, and only then would I claim her completely.

When I sucked on her clit, she gasped. Her thighs pressed against my head, and she ran her fingertips across my horns.

My cock jerked upward, and I almost came from her simple touch alone.

"This is all I'll ever need," I murmured against her clit. "You." I sucked it into my mouth and slid my tongue across it. "This." I started moving my fingers inside her again, my heart thundering when she bucked up to my touch. "And this." With my other hand, I tugged on her nipple, rolling it until it formed a hard bud.

I lifted her hips, splaying her wide for me, and my reward was seeing how she glistened, how nicely she took my fingers. Her passage sucked on my hand, and I couldn't wait to feel it with my cock.

I'd crave this woman forever; I'd never get enough. From the moment I woke until I fell asleep each night—and even in my dreams—I'd want her. Her smiles, the strokes of her hand, and her love.

Whimpers escaped her throat, and I wanted to grin. I was pleasing her, pleasing the one person who mattered the most in the world. It made me want to bellow with joy. Race across the desert. And love her all over again.

"Turren," she cried, lifting her hips to my hand. I pulled my fingers out and replaced them with my tongue, pushing it deep inside her and dragging it across her inner walls when I slid it out. "I'm on fire. Please . . ."

"I've got you, mate. Come for me." I lifted my head only long enough to speak. No way would I be able to stop right now. She tasted like the sweetest fruit. The heat of her was driving *me* wild.

"All I can think of is you, Kaila." I punctuated my words with a stab of my tongue deep inside her. I rolled her clit with one hand while my other stroked her breasts one after the other. Back and forth because I couldn't bear not to give them equal love. "From the moment I wake." Damn, she tasted good. It was all I could do to focus. Soon, I'd feel her around my cock, but was I greedy for wanting this just as much? "Until the time I fall asleep." I added my fingers, pushing them in when my tongue slid out, driving her body to the edge.

And beyond.

Her passage tightened around my tongue, and I tasted her bliss when she came. She jerked upward, riding her pleasure, riding my mouth.

Until she collapsed on the purple leaves and her legs splayed wide.

"I'm limp," she said with a bubbly laugh. "But I bet you're nowhere limp yourself, my wonderful mate."

Rising, she took me by the shoulders and guided me down to lay on the soft vegetation.

"My turn." She licked her lips as she took in my cock throbbing against my abs. "I wonder how you'll taste. Will you let me feast?"

A pack of ashenclaws could burst into the clearing and I wouldn't see them. Shaydes could chitter in the woods, and I wouldn't hear them. All I'd be able to focus on was my precious mate.

She kissed my chest and moved down across my belly, her lips tickling and bringing out my laugh. Even that movement made my cock jerk upward, thickening and hardening to the point I almost couldn't bear it.

She sent me a sultry smile. "What should I do next with you, my beautiful orc mate?"

CHAPTER 29

KAILA

"Whatever you please."

He lay splayed on the ground before me, and I drank in the sight. He *was* beautiful, so perfectly sculpted by the fates themselves.

I couldn't resist touching him.

I stroked his chest, thrilled by the play of muscles beneath my touch. But his cock was waiting, and I couldn't wait to see what it was like to be with a male in such a way. Sliding my hands down his body, I paused to tease my fingertips across the sharp cords of his belly. His golden green skin twitched beneath my touch, and his lips curled up around one of his tusks. He'd closed his eyes to savor every moment.

There wasn't any part of him I loved more than another, but when I got to his cock, I sat back on my heels for a moment to just stare at it. It wasn't a work of art like him or this meadow. It was too big and too thick, corded and with veins, plus the irregular nubs along the surface. But it had a beauty of its own that stunned me.

When I wrapped my hand around it, his groan ripped out.

"Kaila," he breathed, his voice low and husky. "You . . ."

"Tell me what feels good." I used his words, but I needed to know. I hadn't touched a man like this before; I'd never wanted to. Now I couldn't resist. If he didn't enjoy it, I wanted to learn what brought him pleasure and then do it for him.

That was love for you. I'd sacrifice anything just to make sure he was happy, to bask in his smile and feel the stroke of his fingers across my brow.

"Keep touching me. Stroking me," he growled. "Like that."

I slid my fingers all the way up his length, squeezing gently. When I reached the top, I couldn't resist touching the wetness I found there.

His hips jerked up, and he hissed. "Yes, like that, mate. My wonderful, amazing mate."

"I've just gotten started," I said with a smile, feeling emboldened to try more. Leaning down close, I ran my tongue across the tip.

His eyes snapped open, and they literally smoldered. "You . . ." His words dissolved when I sucked him into my mouth.

He tasted salty and sweet all at the same time, so amazing I wanted to keep sucking and drinking from him for hours.

I wanted him to fall apart like I'd done for him. His joy and his body were mine, and I was going to claim them. Only after that would I demand he give me this cock in every way possible.

As I ran my mouth up and down his cock, flicking my tongue across the tip to suck down his juices, my core throbbed. I clenched my thighs together, trying to hold myself back, because I was worried I'd come purely from bringing him pleasure.

His smaller cock—his *spur*—thrust up behind his bigger cock, and when I teased my fingers down it while still sucking on the other, he bellowed.

I lifted my mouth only long enough to speak. "Good?"

His feral gaze locked on mine, and I suspected it wouldn't be long before he was plunging himself inside me.

When I licked his cock again and squeezed his spur, he bolted upright, grasped my shoulders and dragged me up his body claim my mouth with his. I tasted him as well as myself, something that should give me pause, but there was something arousing about the mix of us both.

He'd brought me to complete joy twice. I wasn't sure anything could get better than this.

But when he lowered me to my hands and knees

and moved around behind me, I suspected I was going to find out.

"You, mate," he rasped, clutching my hips. "You . . ."

I grinned, my face pressed into the purple plants, drinking in their scent while he rubbed the head of his cock back and forth, coating it in my wetness.

I was out of control, gasping and pressing back against his cock, needing to feel it driving within me. Heat flew across my skin. Whimpering, I rocked back, breaking free of his hands to meet each of the glides of his cock across my flesh.

"Hold on, my needy mate," he said, humor bubbling in his voice. He gripped my hips again, bracing my body with his big orc hands, then placed the head of his cock at my entrance.

"Yes, yes," I hissed.

A jerk of his hips, and he drove the head of his cock inside me.

I cried out. It felt so good. So big, and the stretch . . . I wasn't sure I could bear the sting but when he pulled out and pressed back within me again, I knew I would. I had to. If he stopped now, I was going to shriek and beg him to finish, to plunge everything he had inside me.

Leaning over me, he rocked his hips, pulling out and pushing back in, each drive sinking his rod deeper.

Until I could feel everything, so long and thick and filling me completely.

"Mate," he growled in my ear. "Mate."

When something—yes, his spur—latched onto my clit, I nearly came in an instant. But I wanted more, so much more. I made my heat back down, go away until I was ready.

He started moving, pumping slowly, exquisitely inside me, to the point it was so beautiful I wanted to cry.

But I was a needy thing, and I needed heavy thrusts to complete me.

"Faster," I cried.

His low laugh rang out. "You're my precious mate, my needy mate. I have everything you're craving." He did, and he gave it to me, hitching his hips back before jerking them forward again, driving that glorious cock all the way to the hilt while his smaller one brought my clit to a fever pitch.

Pleasure erupted inside me, coursing through my veins like living flames. I cried out and moved back to meet his thrusts, my body driving high. I was going to fall apart from the beauty of this moment.

I gripped the vegetation tightly, holding myself in place while he plunged in and out of me, taking me all the way to the top and then pushing me for more, urging me all the way to the sky.

And when I came, the sensations wracked my entire body. I gasped and moaned into the flowers while his cock seemed to thicken inside me.

When my body finally stopped shuddering, and I

wasn't sure I could take any more, he pulsed deep within me, bathing my inner walls with his inner fire.

His hoarse cry echoed in the meadow, and he slumped over me, his body giving into bliss.

WE DOZED, made love again, then slept some more. Finally, in the late afternoon, we made our way back upriver. We stopped to swim, splashing each other and laughing, savoring just being together.

When he held me close and his fingers roamed, I laid back in the water and let him take me again. He claimed me so sweetly that it made me want to cry. I shouted out, a hoarse shout of pleasure that echoed around us.

Finally, as the sun started to set, we knew we had to leave. We ate as we returned to Airest, finding him placidly dozing in the open area where we'd left him.

In no time, we were flying again.

And when Turren's fingers started to roam across my body, I squirmed out of my undergarment, lifted my body above his, and with his guidance, I dropped down on his cock.

While Airest flew on, oblivious to what we were doing on his back, I claimed my mate like he'd done so many times with me.

And after, I slept in his arms, feeling complete for the first time in my life.

We flew all night and by dawn, we'd reached the edge of the forest. My clan's mountain home was still far away, but we'd rest before flying farther. After we arrived, I'd send someone back for Brunnen.

I guided Airest down to the ground to land, and we slid off him. Then I took my mate's hand and led her across the scraggly earth that soon gave way to the sand of the vast desert.

"Wow," she said as she stared, shielding her eyes from the sun.

"I know it doesn't look like much yet." I kicked the scruff with my foot. "But you'll soon see its beauty."

"It's huge. So . . . sandy."

I couldn't tell what she was thinking. I had so much to say but once again, I couldn't find the right words to use. Kaila was everything to me. It was all I could do to convince her to come to my desert home with me.

I'd hidden something from her, something as vital in my life as her.

Once I explained, would she understand and still love me? There would be no hiding it. Soon, it would be revealed, and then I'd know. I'd decided to tell her when we reached my clan. I'd watch her face, praying to the fates that she'd nod and tell me it would be alright. That she accepted this like she had everything else.

No matter what, I'd remain strong. It would rip me asunder to lose her but . . . I had no choice. There was no following a different path than the one I'd laid out before I went to the hunt.

But there would be no hiding my pain if she rejected me.

I had to believe she'd understand, that she wouldn't . . . toss me aside like my parents had.

"You seem sad," she said, sliding her arm through mine and leaning into my side. "Is everything alright?

I could tell her now, but silence had been my way for so long, I wasn't sure how to find my way out of it.

"Everything is fine." Turning, I held her for a long moment before tilting her face up and meeting her gaze. I found trust there. She'd overcome her fear and was eager to face this new challenge by my side.

With a growl, I let it go. It would work out. She'd

see and understand and then I wouldn't need to fear this any longer.

"How long does Airest need to rest?" she asked with a soft smile. She stroked my chest, and my cock immediately responded to her gentle touch.

"Long enough." Sweeping her up into my arms, I carried her into the woods. I found a soft spot and carefully lowered her to the ground, following.

Then I loved her as if this would be the last time, with desperation and the love expanding my heart.

WE REMAINED on the edge of the woods for many hours until Airest had rested enough to carry us to the vox hunting grounds.

"How long will we travel?" Kaila asked.

"About seven hours. More than halfway through the night. In the cooler months, we live near the oasis, but my clan will have moved to the vox mating grounds by now. They'll be settling in when we arrive." A time of change, but perhaps a time for hope as well.

"It's beautiful," she said, gazing out into the desert with the sun low on the horizon. "I've never seen anything prettier in my life than the gold, orange, and red beams cutting across the tan desert sand."

I wrapped my arms around her from behind,

holding her as the sun hitched lower, until it winked out.

"I guess we should go." She shot me a smile. In her eyes, I read excitement. She wasn't afraid any longer.

She trusted me.

May I always be worthy of that trust.

I helped her up onto Airest, and the vox fluttered his wings.

"He's eager to be home." I joined her on the beast's spine, wrapping my arm around her.

"I bet you're eager to be home too."

"I am. There's . . ." Why couldn't I speak the words?

"What?"

"Nothing." With a nudge of my heels, Airest took flight. He flew up over the scruffy land on the edge of the desert and with my guidance, soared above the desert itself. Tipping his head back, he released a squawk.

"See? He just said he can't wait to reach the breeding grounds," she said with a laugh.

"Is that what he said?" Leaning forward, I kissed her cheek, her neck.

She released a shiver and pressed back against my chest, sighing. "You make me feel amazing, Turren. Safe and loved."

"As you should. I adore you. Remember that no matter what."

"I will. I can't wait to see where we'll live and meet all your friends. How many orcs live in your clan?"

"One hundred and three."

"So many. I never considered that there might be more orcs than those living in the forest near my village, let alone that I'd meet them someday. I've heard rumors about a great orc city, but no one I know has ever seen it."

"It's as real as my clan. As me."

"I'm nervous, of course. But for some reason, I'm not worried that they'll accept me. Maybe seeing how much Dakur loves Nia and Pulost adores Mavileen, plus how everyone seems happy to see orcs and humans together has eased that fear. Or I've finally learned how to let go and trust. Finally." Her voice lifted. "Finally!"

Airest squawked again as if he understood, and maybe he did.

"They will love you as much as me." Of this, I had no doubts. How could they do anything less? Each mate one of us brought to the clan was another precious piece of our future. Mates brought hope that our people would not die out.

We flew through the night, and I was grateful she slept. I held her with worry gnawing at my bones. Should I wake her and tell her? No, I would share this with her in the morning. We'd been traveling for a very long time. She needed this rest.

Everything could wait until the morning.

Finally, the lights of my clan winked ahead. Our homes had been constructed on the side of the mountain. The voxes lived above us in aeries leading to a network of cave systems within the mountain itself. That was where they bred and laid their seeds before returning to the clans and orcs they'd left. They'd always lived here.

But while they'd birth the seeds of their young, they didn't raise them. Only when an orc first bonded with a vox had the custom started and continued until this day.

Seeing how close to home we were, Airest found new energy and flew faster. My precious mate continued to sleep, secure in my arms. She didn't wake when Airest landed, and I slid from his spine with her in my arms. Not when I softly spoke with an orc who'd make sure Airest was cared for and released to his aerie. And not when I carried her down the slope and into my home.

I laid her on my bed and quickly stripped, joining her on the soft furs.

I curled around her, and I slept.

Waking at dawn, I stretched.

"When did we arrive?" Kaila sat up, watching my face. Her fingertip traced down my chest, and I was flooded with warmth and love for her once more.

"During the night. You were asleep so I carried you here. Welcome home, my bold mate."

"Bold, eh?" Her lips curled up, and she leaned over to give me a kiss that soon turned to moans.

I rolled her onto her back, and I loved her, praying

to the fates it would not be for the last time.

After, I took her through the back panel in my home and into the heart of the mountain, to the warm pools where my people bathed. I found an isolated one where we could be alone. Once she was ready, I'd present her to my clan.

We dried our bodies and got dressed.

"I'll take you to the people in my clan who make clothing today. They'll create a full wardrobe for you and will have a few items you can wear right away."

She looked down at her skirt and blouse. She'd only brought a few outfits when she fled the village and while they'd been washed in the river, they were getting worn from her travels. "That would be amazing." She gave me a hug. "Thank you."

"For what?" I cupped her pretty face and couldn't resist giving her a kiss. I would've done more if I wasn't worried someone might walk in on us. Next time, I'd mark the cave to show it was occupied. Then I could show my mate how much I adored her.

"For being you."

"I'm your mate. I love you." She stroked my cheek. "That's all that matters."

"You're right. Let me take you to the dining area where we all eat together." I felt better about this already. She was happy here already. Nothing would change this.

I had nothing to fear.

"Wonderful," she said. "I'm starving."

Taking her hand, I led her back to our home and out through the front door.

Orcs passed us, welcoming me back and shooting Kaila happy smiles.

"My mate," I told them all with a grin. "My Kaila."

"There are so many names," she said softly as we walked across the central area, stopping to introduce her multiple times. "I'll do my best to remember them all."

"We're a patient people. Have no fear. Eventually you'll remember."

She shot me a smile that warmed me through. "Love you, mate," she said softly.

"Love you too." I couldn't resist kissing her again.

And I would tell her as soon as I found—

"There you are," someone said, and we broke apart, sharing a smile. "I heard you'd returned, Turren."

"This—" I started to say.

She stopped in front of us, taking in me holding Kaila's hand while juggling an orcling on her hip. "Who is this?"

"My precious mate, Kaila." I turned to my mate, noting the welcoming smile on her face. "Kaila? This is Ferella. And this little one." My fingers shook as I stroked her sweet orcling face. "This is Sianna."

Sianna fussed and held her arms out to me, straining to get away from Ferella.

"Da da," she cried.

CHAPTER 31

KAILA

Turren had a child. A beautiful little girl. And the orc female holding her had to be . . .

"Why didn't you tell me?" The hurt roaring through my chest made it difficult to breathe.

He looked at me in dismay. "I was going to. Soon." His arms lifted to take Sianna from Ferella, and Ferella backed away.

"You have a mate? A mate." Ferella sighed and shook her head. "Perhaps you should've sent word? But welcome back. She's missed you." After giving me a nod, she strode around Turren and handed the orcling to me. "Here you are. She will love her new mama."

I floundered, juggling the little girl who took one look at me and started to wail. She held her arms out to Turren, and he took her from me. Sianna stared at me, sniffing while stuffing her fingers into her mouth, shrieking around them.

"I'm so glad you're back," Ferella said. "Let me know if you need any more help." Leaving us, she strode across the compound and entered one of the wooden homes built into the side of the hill.

"We need to talk," Turren said over Sianna's wails.

Great. My mate had . . . Well, he'd told me he slept with someone. Ferella? Back then might've been a good time to tell me that the two of them . . .

All of this was a farce. He didn't need me, not when he had Ferella waiting for him here in his clan.

After sending him a glare, I raced toward our home —*his* home.

"Kaila, wait," he called out, but I ignored him. "You're right! I should've told you."

Why hadn't he?

His omission . . . hurt. Because it showed a lack of trust, the trust I'd extended to him when I agreed to give up the future I'd planned to follow him to a new home. Here, I was among strangers, and this was a completely different way of life.

Tears streamed down my face as I rushed to the back wall and wrenched open the door. After slamming the panel closed behind me, I hurried down the slope leading into the mountain and soon got lost among all the caves holding steaming pools. I passed a few orcs who gave me odd looks and kept going, walking for what felt like hours.

Finally, I came to a large cavern with a waterfall cascading down the far wall. It splashed into a large pool that narrowed to snake along the left side of the cave before disappearing into a hole low on the wall. Vines coated the walls and draped from the ceiling, their pale yellow and pink flowers perfuming the steamy air. Whisps coated the upper parts of the room, their tiny lights peeking out from behind the vegetation.

I sunk on the mossy shore and stared at the vast pool, tossing pebbles into the water. Tears continued to fall down my face, and I wasn't sure what to do. My world had been shaken once more, but the person I thought I could trust the most wasn't here with me. He'd withheld something vital about his life.

Stretching out my legs, I lay back on the soft ground, listening to the fall of the water. It soothed the turmoil churning inside me.

Someone sat beside me, and I didn't need to open my eyes to know who it was.

I kept them closed because . . . I couldn't bear to look at him right now. But I spoke. "I talked about raising my brother. I told you how hard it was to be a mother to a little boy who sobbed all the time when he was three and I was twelve. That might've been the time to tell me about Sianna." And Ferella, but I wasn't going there yet.

"You're right," he said softly. "I'm sorry."

I nodded. I was sure he was. Sitting up, I stared at

the water. I still couldn't look at my mate. "I told you everything I wanted for my future, how I hoped to build a new life. That would've also been a wonderful time for you to say, *hey, a little orcling girl who calls me da da is waiting for me back at my clan. I can't wait for you to meet her.* Instead, you said nothing." And again, I didn't bring up Ferella.

"Yes. I . . . I thought of telling you, but each time I wanted to begin, I remembered how you said you weren't sure you wanted a child, how you felt you'd already been a parent, that if you decided you wanted an orcling with me, you'd tell me."

"Don't try to blame me for not telling me something as vital as this. You have a *daughter*."

"Actually, Sianna is not my true child."

Now that, I hadn't expected. "You said you and another orc female were together once. That's all it takes to create an orcling. I assume she's the result of that relationship with Ferella."

"Ferella's just a friend. A different orc female and I *were* together. But Sianna is my brother and his mate's child."

Hold on. I turned to face him. "She's not your child? And Ferella . . ."

"Has been caring for Sianna while I was away. As far as I'm concerned, she *is* my child. I'm raising her as my own. When my brother and his mate were killed, Ferella offered to help me with their orcling. She has no mate of her own and wanted to do all she could for the poor orphan child."

My sigh leaked out. "I'm not hurt about Sianna. She's adorable. I'd be . . . her stepmother and there's no way I can do anything less than love her." I swallowed, and it went down hard. "I'm sorry if I gave you the impression I wouldn't welcome a child into my life."

"It's not your fault. I know this. I should've told you everything, should've given you the chance to get used to the idea. I guess I worried that you'd reject me like my parents did. They adored my brother but . . . they essentially ignored me after I was injured. I didn't want to give you any reason to tell me you didn't want to be with me like they did."

"What would you do if I told you I didn't want to raise Sianna?"

"A clan raises a child, not just a parent."

"The thing is, you didn't give me a chance. You decided I would reject her like your parents rejected you. You made that decision for me rather than let me make it for myself." I rose to my feet, staring into his eyes. "That's what hurts. That you chose to be dishonest with me about something as important as this. That little girl is a big part of your life and your future. I still can't understand why you didn't tell me."

Turning, I started walking back the way I'd come.

"Kaila, wait."

I couldn't. Pain kept crashing through me, and it

was all I could see and feel. I knew he was hurting but . . . he'd been dishonest when I needed him to trust me as much as I did him.

I turned to face him, taking the devastation on his face. The same feeling kept ricocheting around inside me. "I need time. Please give me some time."

Pivoting, I took off again. Instead of slowing or waiting for him to walk with me, I broke into a run. I didn't stop until I stood outside his home.

"There you are!" Brunnen rushed over and swept me up in his arms, giving me a hug. "I've been looking for you everywhere. This place is amazing, isn't it?" He set me down and his arm swept out to take in the enormous valley in front of us, ringed by the mountain range. "They said I can be there when the vox seeds open," he gushed. "Some have been laid already and voxes will slip from the seeds in a few months. One will bond with me and . . ." He frowned. "You don't look happy for me."

"Oh, I am," I said brightly. Hooking my arm through his, I urged him to walk, though I didn't know where we were going.

I didn't need to look behind to know that Turren was nearby. I could *feel* him.

I . . . wasn't sure what to say. My life had gone from unsettled to one full of love and a purpose. Now I felt unsettled once more. I wasn't going to torture him. I loved him, and we were meant to be together.

I just needed some time to think.

"Have they showed you where you're staying yet?" I asked.

"I thought with you, but Daskin told me many of the young males share housing near the central compound. He told me that you and Turren would make me welcome but that his home was small. I hope you don't mind that I told him I want to stay with the young males for now." He looked at me with so much concern, I hugged him.

"I love that idea."

"I was just going to get something to eat," he said. "I'll tell you more about it."

"Sure, I'll join you."

"Is Turren hungry?" Stopping, he looked back. "He's standing there, watching us."

"He and I . . ." I didn't want to lay this on my brother's shoulders, but he'd figure things out fast even if I didn't tell him. "He and I argued. We're going to make this work, but I'm taking a small break for now. If it's all right with you, we can eat alone. Then you can show me where you'll live and maybe where the voxes lay their seeds. I'm curious about how that works, and I can't wait to see everything."

"Alright." Puzzlement was clear on his face, but it cleared. "I don't mind eating with only you. It'll be like when we were living back in the village. And I want to show you the seeds. Maybe one will slip out and bond with you."

"Maybe one will."

We followed others into a larger building in the center of the open area below the homes and got in line with them, shuffling toward a long table where orcs dished up food for each individual. There were a few choices, none of which I'd seen before, but I *had* said I wanted to try new food and now was my chance.

Taking our plates to an empty table, we sat.

Turren got food but didn't join us. He sat by himself at a table some distance away, facing us. He ate, but he didn't look our way.

While everything was tasty, I couldn't eat more than a few bites.

Turren was giving me time, something I told him I needed.

If only this bit of freedom didn't make me feel so sad.

I wanted to go to Kaila, to hold her. I needed to tell her how sorry I was that I hadn't shared everything I should. But she said she needed time to think, and I was going to give this to her. I wouldn't push her or make decisions for her. She had to do this on her own. But I'd wait forever for her. I loved her.

And I would hope the fates would be kind and guide us back together. If they did, I vowed I'd always be honest with her, that I'd spend the rest of my life making up to her for my mistake.

"Where's Sianna?" Ferella stood beside the table with a plate of food.

"She's napping. Urlain is sitting with her." The elder adored my niece and loved taking her for walks and playing with her. She stated it made her feel young. Her own children and grandchildren were grown.

Ferella nodded. "Why aren't you eating with your mate?"

"She's with her brother. She missed him. He had to travel separately and just arrived." Everyone would soon know Kaila and I were mated but not together. Whispers would spread through the clan and I . . .

I realized what I was doing to myself, to my mate and I, and I stopped the thoughts. Other mated couples had disagreements and resolved them. Kaila and I would be no different.

"Normally, I'd offer to sit with you but . . ." Her gaze fell on Daskin, my second in command who'd filled in while I was away.

He wasn't looking at her, but his face darkened as if he felt her touch.

Without saying anything else to me, she strode over and stood on the other side of his table. They spoke, but I couldn't hear what they said. Then she lowered her plate onto the table and sat across from him.

His pendant blazed, as did hers, and conversation cut off in the room. Orcs grinned and someone got up and walked over to Daskin, slapping him on the back. He did the same with Ferella.

I grinned their way, but my smile soon fell. My heart felt empty without Kaila by my side.

Because I didn't want her to think I was following

her everywhere—though I wanted to—I left the dining area after I finished and went to the central building where I met up with Daskin. Ferella followed him inside the small building and leaned against the wall, her gaze locked on him. Their pendants kept blazing, alternating like they were giant stars winking at each other in the night.

"I'll, well, *we'll* need some time off," Daskin said, sending Ferella a big smile. "My new mate and I would like to take some time together."

"Just share what I missed while I was gone and you're free to leave with Ferella after," I said.

"I'm glad you have a new mate, Turren," Ferella said. "She'll be the mother Sianna needs."

I nodded, not wanting to say anything when these two were obviously happy.

Daskin shared some news, but nothing major had happened while I was away. Then he and Ferella left, holding hands. We'd see them again in a week or two, and I wished them well.

I settled in my wooden chair, tipped my head back to stare at the wooden ceiling, and sighed.

CHAPTER 33

KAILA

After eating, Brunnen took me to the large building where many young orc males stayed. Beds were set up inside in a row on one side, with wooden containers for personal possessions at the foot of each.

"You're sure you'll be happy here?" I asked him, though I didn't have any other place to offer. I wasn't even sure where I was going to sleep tonight.

My heart hurt. I missed Turren already. But what could I say to him? He spoke of his difficulty finding words and now it was me who couldn't figure out what words to use to fix this.

"I love it here already," my brother said.

An orc male entered and passed us, smacking Brunnen on the back on the way by.

"We're all going to play gromgret if you're interested," he said.

"This is my friend, Nuark," Brunnen said. "Nuark? This is my sister, Kaila."

"The new mate of our caedos," Nuark said reverently. "Welcome." His face darkened as he hurried through the room, stooping down in front of a trunk.

"I've never played gromgret," Brunnen told me. "I'm not even sure what it is, but..."

He was excited to have a new friend.

"Go join him." I didn't want to hold him back. "We can go to the aerie another time."

He gazed longingly in Nuark's direction. "You're sure? Back in the village, well, I didn't have a lot of friends. They all had each other, and they didn't bother with me."

My heart hurt that I hadn't made an effort to match him with friends. But I was busy working and trying to survive. It never occurred to me. "Go." I nudged his side. "I'm going to look for Turren."

I couldn't stand this. We needed to talk it out; find a way back to each other.

"That's good." Brunnen scratched the back of his neck. "He loves you. I bet he's sorry he upset you."

He was. I knew this. And I was going to tell him. But I looked everywhere for him and couldn't find him. When I asked someone, they said they thought they'd seen him heading out on his vox to fly over the valley. Someone had seen a herd of boolongs and if it was true, Turren was going to put together a hunting party.

Because I really did want to talk with him, I went to our home—and I was going to call it that at all times. This was a bump in our relationship, but I was sure we'd get over it and be stronger on the other side.

Inside, I found an elderly orc female sitting in a chair, humming. Sianna lay on a tiny bed nearby, sound asleep with her fingers stuffed into her mouth.

"Welcome, I'm Urlain," she said. "And you're Kaila, our caedos's new mate." She rose. "I assume you've come here to be with your daughter."

The child was sleeping deeply, releasing soft sighs. I crept forward and stood over her, watching her. "She looks peaceful."

"She's a good orcling. Such a tragedy that her parents died."

"Yes. Turren told me they were killed while traveling."

"Only their precious orcling survived. A hunter heard her crying and investigated. I'm afraid they weren't able to recover her parents' bodies. Such a sorrowful time for their clan and ours."

"Their clan?"

"Yes, the clan Turren grew up in. The one he left when he was fifteen. He came here and became ours." Her probing gaze met mine. "We love him."

"I do too." That would never go away. "When did her parents die?"

Urlain's head tilted. "Turren didn't tell you?"

Not these small details, plus the big one lying on

the fur-covered bed. "We didn't talk much about it."

"It was only four months ago."

"Not long. I'm terribly sorry."

"The fates can be cruel sometimes." She sighed and started toward the front of the building.

I turned, watching her. "Where are you going?"

"I have many things that require my time. If you'd like, I'll come sit with Sianna tomorrow to free you for other tasks. I adore her, and I'm always happy to play with her."

With that, she left.

I dropped into the chair and watched the tiny child sleep. She didn't look any older than my brother when our parents died. My heart was wrenched back to that time, to the endless pain I'd felt about their loss. To my dismay when I realized that, as my brother's only surviving relative, I would be responsible for raising him. No one suggested that a twelve-year-old still needed raising herself. I was old enough to work and women didn't need an education, they said. I could handle it all.

Now I would raise another child, and for some reason, it felt different this time. Perhaps because I was older. Or my heart already couldn't resist this perfect little being.

When she stirred, I picked her up and held her.

She continued to doze, and her sleepy sighs made my heart crack wide open.

I smiled and kissed the top of her head.

CHAPTER 34
TURREN

I didn't return to my mountain home the next day.

Or the day after that.

Or even on the third day after I left.

I felt cowardly for staying away so long. Yes, the boolong herd needed to be studied, but I could've returned the first night and left the rest to the males in my clan to plan the hunt.

Instead of leaving the next morning, however, I stayed with them, hunting and taking down enough of the herd to provide meat for the clan for months. I remained to clean the meat and smoke it. I sat companionably with the other males around the fire in the evening while they sent me confused looks.

I had a new mate. They didn't understand why I'd chosen to be with them instead of her.

Each night, I slept on the ground out in the open alongside them. It was lonely without Kaila.

I missed her so much.

Flying Airest back home on the fourth day, I guided him to his aerie. I rubbed him down and made sure he had food. And when I remained, standing in the corner, visiting with him, I realized what I was doing. Hiding from Kaila wouldn't fix the problem between us. It was time I found her and asked her if she'd had enough time to think.

Leaving the aerie, I strode down the hillside, nodding to those I passed and taking in how gorgeous it was here in the mountains. How cool and crisp the air was, and how much I adored living here. I enjoyed the desert as much, but this was a different kind of beauty. Stark and harsh while still lovely.

When I spied Brunnen leaving the long building where most of the older youngling males lived, laughing with his new orc friends, I walked over to him.

"There you are," he said, grinning to his friends before returning his gaze to me. "You've been gone a long time."

"Yes." I stood there, feeling crazy for remaining away so long.

Another thing I'd need to apologize to Kaila for.

"I was about to go play gromgret," Brunnen said. "It's a lot of fun."

"He scores all the time," one of the other males

grumbled. "He may be thin and lacking in muscles," he nudged Brunnen, who only laughed, "but he's fast. We love having him on the team."

"I'm glad you're having fun," I said, peering around. "Do you know where Kaila is?"

Brunnen shrugged. "I haven't seen her since breakfast. Maybe she's inside the house? She mentioned something about taking Sianna back there for a nap."

"She's . . . with Sianna?"

"Sure. What a cute little orcling she is. We've been eating all our meals together. She even lets me hold her." He stiffened his spine proudly. "I'm an uncle. Did you know that?"

"You are." I was grateful he was so enthusiastic about my daughter.

I'd thought Sianna would be with Urlain all this time while Kaila . . . was thinking.

"Who would've thought me being an uncle would happen so fast? I mean, I believed . . ." Brunnen's face darkened. "You know what I mean."

He assumed he wouldn't be an uncle until Kaila and I had an orcling together. Was there much hope left for that?

I should've come home the first evening. I should've told her I was leaving before I did so, blurted my apologies and dealt with whatever she might say about me raising a child. So many things I should've done.

Like my parents had said, I was a complete failure.

But then I remembered how Urlain welcomed me into this clan, how she'd spoken up when the prior caedos got old and stated she was stepping down. How Urlain told the others I'd be a good leader.

Perhaps I wasn't a failure after all, not in this part of my life.

"Anyway, I've got to go." With a nod to me, Brunnen hurried down the hillside, catching up with the others heading toward the flat open area where younglings played the game.

I strode to our home and paused outside, listening. Was that soft singing I heard inside? Holding my breath, I stepped into the small open area. I found Kaila sitting in the chair near the side window, her back facing me. She held Sianna, and there wasn't any sight prettier than that. She stroked Sianna's back and my daughter slept, her fingers in her mouth for sucking.

Kaila must've heard me shut the door, because she looked over her shoulder. Her eyes and her expression didn't change.

Did I still see love there, though? I wasn't sure what I'd do if she told me she didn't want to be with me anymore.

That was why I'd stayed away. As long as I was hunting and sleeping beside my clansmales at night, there was still a chance I'd have Kaila in my life when I returned.

Mates could reject the other. It had happened,

though not for so long that I couldn't remember exactly who had done so.

But it wasn't unheard of.

"You're back." She rose and laid Sianna on her bed to sleep. She stroked the orcling's forehead and the smile she gave my daughter made everything inside me come to a sudden halt.

"You love her," I croaked.

"How could I not when she's a part of you?"

I strode over and dropped to my knees in front of her. "I'm sorry. I love you. I'm sorry."

"Turren." Her face creasing with pain, Kaila took my hands and tugged on them. "Up. Please don't kneel."

"I love you. I'll grovel forever as long as you tell me we stand a chance of being together again." When I realized what I was doing, I rose to my feet. "I'm sorry again. Here I am, pushing you into saying things that may not be in your heart."

"Turren."

Someone scratched on the door. Kaila walked around me and let Urlain inside.

"Ah, there's my precious one." Urlain hurried over to stand beside Sianna's bed. She turned to face us. "And there are two precious people who I suspect need to talk." With a low laugh, she flicked her hands our way. "Go. Leave me in peace with this sweet orcling. I'll remain with her for as long as you have need."

"Thank you." Kaila went over and stood on her toes to kiss Urlain's wrinkly cheek.

"Now, now." Urlain patted Kaila's back. "Go. Be with your mate. Talk."

She must know things weren't as they should be between us.

After thanking her, Kaila and I left, stopping out front.

Kaila sucked in a breath and released it, looking around. "It's beautiful here. I still can't believe how gorgeous the view is. The mountains. Everything about this part of the world is perfect."

"Would you like to walk together?"

She nodded and started toward the path that wound behind the village. It kept going for many cliks, along the side of the mountains. Did she know this?

"I was away too long," I said as we left the village behind and walked side-by-side on the path worn smooth by generations of footsteps.

"You were. I missed you."

My heart flipped over, and I wasn't sure I'd ever be able to breathe again. "I missed you, my . . ." Stopping, I pinched my eyes shut.

"What's wrong?" She returned to stand in front of me. I didn't see her because my eyes were still closed, but I caught her lovely scent. Heard her breathing. Felt the warmth emanating from her body.

"While we traveled through the forest, I spent a lot of time thinking up new words I could use to describe you, my mate," I said. "I'm not a male who is comfortable with words, but I wanted so much to impress you. I *had* to find them in order to gift them to you."

"You made me growl, and you made me laugh." Her voice bubbled with humor. "There were times when I wanted to smack you, though I didn't."

I opened my eyes to find her looking up at me, though I still couldn't read the expression on her face. "You should've smacked me. I often deserved it."

"I understand why you held things back. I forgive you if that's what you need, but inside here," she reached up to tap my chest, "I'm not sure you'll believe me."

"I told you my family died, but I didn't share anything else." Taking her hand, I led her a bit farther down the path until we came to an area where it was wider. Someone had long ago crafted a stone bench and placed it near the cliff on the left. Many times, I'd sat there and looked out at the view, thinking about all the ways I could be a good caedos.

Now I sat with my mate beside me, thinking about how I could be a better mate.

She swung her legs that didn't reach the ground and remained silent. She was waiting.

It was time for me to find the words that kept pushing against the inside of my heart. If I held them inside much longer, I'd not only risk losing the only female I'd ever love, but I'd also never be the person I'd always wanted to be.

"We talked a little bit about my arm," I said.

"It's smaller than the other. Less muscled. Many scars. Such a horrible injury."

"It's not as strong as my right arm. As I said, an animal attacked me, nearly ripping it off. I was young, and I don't remember much other than the pain. So much pain. After I'd healed, I was supposed to exercise my arm to make it form like the other as I grew. But no matter what I did, it didn't happen. I grew bigger but it didn't keep up with my body. I've accepted it'll never do what the other can, that it makes me weak."

"I haven't seen it hold you back once."

"I try very hard to make sure it doesn't." And I hated that she'd noticed it at all. But if I couldn't be vulnerable with the one person I loved above all others, who else would understand? "I didn't grow up in the Ember Clan."

"Urlain mentioned that."

"My parents were part of the Basselt Clan. This clan lives deep beneath a long mountain range many cliks from here. I had a brother, as you knew, and he had a mate."

"How did you end up here?"

"One day, when my father was berating me, telling me how worthless I am, I just . . . ran. I grabbed my staff and nothing else and I bolted. I didn't stop running until I'd left the boundaries of my clan."

"Urlain said you were fifteen when you arrived

here. That's not much older than Burren." She rubbed my arm. "I'm sorry."

I wanted to close my eyes and lean into her touch, but I needed to finish this first. "I made my way toward these mountains and what did I find? A clan who welcomed me. An elder, Urlain, took me in and praised me. She told me my strength lay in my will and my kind heart." I looked toward Kaila, startled to find tears trickling down her face.

"Mate," I croaked, tugging her into my lap and wrapping my arms around her. "I love you. I'm sorry I'm making you cry."

"Turren, stop saying you're sorry." She was weeping harder now. I couldn't do anything to stop it. "Don't keep saying that. You apologized already. I accepted it. I would've told you that night if you hadn't left."

"You would've?"

"I needed time to think but that didn't take long. But by the time I returned to our home, you were already gone."

"Yes. I went hunting with the others."

"I hope it was a good hunt." Humor, pure, wonderful humor shone in her voice. She sniffed through her tears.

"It was. Many boolongs were taken." I cleared my throat, eager to finish. Because I suspected . . . Oh, how I hoped . . . that Kaila wanted to be with me once more.

"When the Ember Clan caedos stepped down two

years ago, Urlain told me I had to take over the position. I was thirty by then and in my heart, this was my clan."

"You did it."

"Yes. My people, my clan approved. Everyone. And just like that, I was no longer rejected. I had a purpose and value."

"You'll always have value. It's what's in your heart that truly matters."

"You're right. I know this. It's just very hard to accept it."

"I understand." She sighed. "Then your parents and your brother and his mate died. All of them except Sianna."

"Would you believe my first clan brought her to me? They said I had the right to raise her, though they would love to take her back to the Basselt Clan if I didn't. How could I say no? She's perfect. I love her very much."

"She is." Kaila snuggled against my chest. "So where does this leave us now?"

Where *did* it leave us? "I love you and want to be with you. I'll always feel this way. But I'll never pressure you or make choices for you again."

She turned in my embrace and wrapped her legs around me, looking up at me. "I want to be with you, Turren. I want to love you from the moment you wake until you lay your head beside mine at dusk and all the time in between. I want to raise Sianna and any orclings we might have together, and I want to stand proudly by your side. The side of my clan caedos."

"Mate," I said. "My wonderful, perfect, glorious, fabulous mate."

Her lips curled up. "Only wonderful, perfect, glorious, and fabulous? What else?"

"There are many words I hold within my heart still to name you," I said solemnly.

"I can't wait to hear them."

I kissed her. Held her. And I knew then that I was enough for Kaila.

And that was all that mattered.

CHAPTER 35
EPILOGUE 1
KAILA

Three Months Later

We strode up the hill toward the aerie. Brunnen held Sianna's hand as she toddled along with us. She gazed up at him raptly. She adored her uncle. Adored me. And she was the sweetest little girl ever. I couldn't imagine not having her in our lives.

Today, however, some vox seeds were ripe to hatch, and everyone interested in bonding with a vox would be there to see if the fates selected them for this honor.

"Excited, my vigorous mate?" Turren asked from

beside me. His arm was around my back, warm and strong.

I winked up at him and spoke in a low voice only he'd hear. "I believe *you're* the vigorous mate today."

We'd made love, and he'd experimented with new positions that required strength on his side and contortions on mine. My body still hummed, and I couldn't wait to be back inside our snug home to try some things I'd envisioned since we left.

We'd expanded our home to include a private space for us. Now we didn't need to worry about disturbing Sianna while she slept.

"Perhaps I am vigorous," he said with a smile.

He'd settled into himself and was even happier now than when we made up and celebrated our love. As always, his arm bothered him, though soaking in the hot pools and massage helped. But he no longer tried to hide it or what happened in his past. He'd learned to accept it and focused on his strengths rather than his perceived weaknesses.

And I couldn't love him more than I did right now.

We reached the top of the path and paused to look out over the valley. Once the vox seeds hatched, many of the clan would begin the process of packing our things to move to the oasis for the cooler months. Those who bonded would remain behind, though only long enough to solidify the connection. Then they'd bring their voxes to the oasis to continue their training.

Brunnen, of course, was very eager to bond with a vox. He'd made friends, and he loved it here. We both fit in seamlessly, something that had never happened back in the village I grew up in. I wasn't an orc, but this was my place, my very soul.

"So beautiful," I sighed as I took in the sweeping valley full of every shade of green and blue. The leaves on many of the trees were turning red, orange, and yellow, and soon, some would drop, leaving the skeletal frame dormant until spring. The sun peeked above the mountain range on the other side of the valley, making everything glow. "I don't think I'll ever get used to seeing this place."

Turren put his arms around me from behind and curled forward to kiss my cheek. "We'll be back. Wait until you see the valley in the spring. So many rich colors. And the fruit! We'll eat well all next summer."

Then we'd leave again for the desert in the fall. I suspected I'd love traveling, not just to explore a new part of our world, but to savor the differences of each one.

"Come on," Brunnen said, his feet shifting on the rock soil. "They'll slide from their seeds soon and if I'm not there, the one meant for me will pick another." He'd fretted so much about this over the past month.

"Coom en," Sianna lisped, and they both laughed.

"If a new vox is your fate-chosen bond, then it won't pick anyone else," Turren said. He took my hand and led me over to the opening in the vast cave system spread across this part of the mountain. Openings along the sides allowed the voxes to come and go, and inside was a network of aeries where they rested at night.

Farther in, we'd find large caverns where the voxes bred. And in the center of a few of the caverns, seeds slowly matured until they stretched their pods to the point they'd separate and release the baby vox. The base of each cavern was covered in thick vegetation, and the babies would remain there, eating and growing until they were big enough to fly. I was told the oasis offered a similar plant, making it easy to take a bonded vox with us.

They actually loaded the tiny beasts into carts and used tame boolongs to pull it. There was some talk of capturing some boolong young and penning them to raise and breed. Then we would selectively use some for meat and save the effort of hunting.

I planned to start a big garden not only near the oasis but when we returned to the mountains in the spring. Turren told me he'd take me to a village on the edge of the desert to buy seeds.

We entered the mountainside through a large opening at the head of the path and paused to let our eyes adjust. Whisps peppered the ceiling, and someone lifted a large leaf from an enormous tree growing in the valley. When he started sweeping it through the air, he generated a breeze that coasted across the whisps and made them glow brighter to light our way.

We walked to the right and down a long slope, Sianna toddling between Brunnen and me. She kept pointing and laughing, and we couldn't help but chuckle along with her.

Turren scooped her up and placed her on his shoulders. She latched onto his horns and wiggled, urging him with squeals to run down the slope—which he did while making grunts like he was a ferocious beast.

Brunnen shook his head and we hurried to keep pace with them.

The path ended at a cavern with a raised area in the center where the voxes had laid their seeds. Other caverns could be reached through openings along the walls, but this cavern was reserved for the Ember Clan.

Ten seeds stood in a circle, and we strode down another path and through the vegetation to get to the spot where we'd wait.

Orcs would stoon start arriving from other clans and each had a cavern with seeds assigned to them.

I couldn't wait to see Dakur and Nia again, and to meet some of the other women who'd mated with orcs. Mid-summer, we planned to travel to the orc city on the sea to visit old friends and meet new ones.

We stopped, milling about with the other orcs eager to bond with a vox this season.

"How will we know if one has chosen us?" I whispered.

"You'll know." Turren jostled Sianna around to hold in his arms. She gazed raptly at the seeds and kicked her legs.

"It's starting to happen," someone cried out.

Orcs standing along the wall cheered, their arms lifted overhead.

I couldn't see over all the tall orcs in front of me. Brunnen wormed his way to the front, but he was thirteen. No one had a problem with a boy doing something like that. But if both of us did it . . . I was the mate of the clan caedos. While no one expected formal behavior from me, I wanted to represent my mate well.

Seeing my dilemma, Turren shifted Sianna to his left arm and swept me up with his right, holding me easily at his eye level. Now I could see! And I adored him for seeing my need and answering simply, so he got a steamy kiss.

The seeds started shifting, rocking, tugging my attention in that direction. Sometimes, they didn't split, and one of the orcs would have to finish opening it with a weapon, but it looked like they'd all split wide today.

A hush fell over the cavern. Would all the new vox young pick someone to bond with? Some didn't. They'd mature without a bonded person and fly freely throughout the mountains. I'd seen them soaring in packs high above.

One of the seeds toppled over, splitting when it landed, and a vox baby slipped out. It rose to its feet, wobbling, and peered around. Flapping its wings, it squawked and stumbled off the platform and over to Brunnen.

He gasped and held his hands toward it, and I swore I could see shimmering threads stretching between them.

My brother burst into tears. So did I.

"Let me down, love," I whispered, and Turren complied. On my feet, I made my way to my brother and put my arm around him.

"Are you alright?" I asked.

He nodded, unable to look away from the vox. "It's happening. This is . . . Her name is Clessa."

Clessa peered at me but returned her attention to Brunnen. He stooped down, wiping his eyes, and stroked her face. She was a perfectly formed vox, only much smaller, though nearly as big as my brother. I'd heard they grew quickly, feasting on the lush vegetation growing in this cavern.

Turren joined us, nodding in approval when Brunnen looked his way.

"Oh, my surprised mate?" he suddenly said.

I looked up at him, my eyebrows rising. "*Surprised?*"

He tilted his head to the right . . . A tiny blue vox stood nearby, looking up at me. It flapped its wings

AVA ROSS

and released a shrill cry, and I *knew*. I felt the bond form between us, strong and beautiful.

I dropped to my knees and held out my arms. It toddled over and nudged my belly with its snout.

"I've got a vox, mate." I grinned up at Turren through my tears. "His name is Weslain."

Turren rubbed my shoulder. "That's a wonderful name." He bent down and kissed my cheek, his arm going around me.

Sitting on his opposite thigh, Sianna chortled and kicked her legs.

And with Turren's arm around me, I began bonding with my new baby vox.

CHAPTER 36

EPILOGUE 2

KAILA

Six Months Later

Tonight, we'd attend the Flame Dance Festival in the orc city. We'd arrived a few days ago and were staying with Madr and Lyneth in their mountain estate. I'd brought Weslain because I couldn't bear to leave him, and he was growing so fast, he'd soon be flying. Not carrying me, yet, but soon.

My brother had remained behind in our clan's mountain home to continue working with Clessa. Sianna had come with us, flying with us.

"Ready to leave, my special mate?" Turren asked. Earlier, we'd flown on Airest to the palace. I couldn't believe we were staying here tonight. Tomorrow, we'd fly back to Madr and Lyneth's estate.

And tonight, we'd attend the Flame Dance Festival being held in the center of the city.

"Yes, I'm ready." I'd joined the other women mated to orcs in a large sitting room while Turren visited with his male friends. We'd sipped fillawate and laughed about all the antics our mates and children got up to.

"Enjoy yourself," Urlain said from the other side of the room where she sat with all the children gathered around her. Zur, Eleri and Odik's oldest son sat nearby, intently listening to each word she spoke. He was the keeper of stories for their sea clan, and he wanted to memorize some tales from the Ember Clan while Urlain was here.

"Behave," Rhoslyn told Shirra, her words echoed by Eleri to her daughter, Yusta. She handed her and Jaus's new infant daughter to one of the palace staff. An orc female had been assigned to care for each orcling, and we had plenty of them here tonight.

Sianna sat near Urlain, listening to the story. Seeing me getting ready to leave, she rose and rushed over to hug my knees. I picked her up and kissed both of her cheeks while she laughed.

"My girl is getting so big," I exclaimed, and she laughed harder. This child was the joy not only of Turren and my life, but our entire clan. She made everyone smile just by being near her.

"Big, big!" she cried, wiggling to get down. When I placed her on the floor, she went over to sit with Yusta and Shirra, her new friends she adored.

In four months' time, she'd have a little brother or sister. My baby bump was just big enough for her to stroke and talk to the orcling inside, something she adored doing each night before going to bed.

"Feeling well?" Turren asked, wrapping his arms around me from behind. He stroked my belly.

We couldn't wait to hold our special person in our arms.

"Very. I'm looking forward to dancing."

"Dakur and I have a special surprise for tonight," Nia said from where she sat with Dakur on a sofa. She stroked his thigh and rubbed her belly. She was due to deliver at any time. She'd talked about not going tonight but decided to attend. If she got tired, she and Dakur would leave early.

"What is it?" Alwen asked in excitement. She held their baby girl, Beline, on her lap and would pass her to the attentive orc female standing nearby. Rising, she leaned into Zickar's side. "Is it something to eat? Because I'm hungry!"

Pregnant again already, she had a voracious appetite, something that both amazed and astounded me since she wasn't a huge person to begin with.

"It's not food," Nia said with a wink. "You'll see."

Since we were walking together to the festival, we left the children in capable orc hands and went down to the front to gather. We sat on benches, waiting for Jaus, the orc king, to arrive. He didn't take long, striding out through the front door with his attendants following. He strode over to Rhoslyn, lifted her, and gave her a long kiss. She moaned and clung to his shoulders.

It was like that for all of us. Even now, after years together, Eleri and Odik would sneak off to be alone together, leaving us to watch their children for a short time.

Madr and Lyneth shared a love of cooking and had been preparing all our meals, laughing and teasing each other as they worked in the estate's kitchen.

As for Alwen and Zickar, they ran the Matis Clan smoothly, sharing the duties and their love with each other and with their people.

And while shadows sometimes lurked in Nia's eyes, when she looked Dakur's way, she literally glowed. I could tell they'd love each other forever, just like me and Turren.

We started walking down the road. In the distance, cries of joy rang out. Jaus explained about the festival as we strode together. Already, I could see street performers ahead, dressed in bright costumes. They danced and swayed among the vendors selling food on sticks we could buy if we got hungry.

A fire blazed ahead in the city square. Sparks coiled up to the sky, and I could feel the heat radiating from it already.

"The festival represents the unity of our people," Jaus said, smiling down at Rhoslyn. "All the clans, not just ours, will send orcs here tonight."

"And don't forget those coming from the human village," she said. "Ten women!"

"You got them to agree?" Alwen asked.

"As you know, I've gone back to the village a few times now to speak with the women. They're slowly coming around to the idea that orcs make good husbands." She smiled up at Jaus and squeezed his hand. "Some of you who I won't name can be intimidating—"

"Not me," he growled, and we all laughed. He put on a strong front, but he was a sweetie inside. Everyone adored him, and it was clear he ran the city well.

"Never you," she breathed before continuing. "The women gathered at the village and made their demands. The men balked at first, but we have ways of making them cooperate." She nodded toward me. "For one thing, the mate hunts will continue but only with volunteers."

Such an amazing idea. No one should feel afraid to seek an orc husband. And no one should be forced to leave the village unless it was something they wanted.

"Twenty orcs, four from each clan, are taking jobs in the village," she said as we turned a corner and started down the last street leading to the center of the city where the bonfire and dancing waited. "This will give everyone a chance to get to know orcs better and a chance for women to see that orcs can make superior partners."

"Which they do," Lyneth said, smiling at Madr.

"I'm sure we'll hear about matings soon," Rhoslyn said. "But if nothing else, the mate hunt will change for the better."

"I love this," Eleri said in a dreamy voice. "It's perfect."

"The best outcome for all of us," Rhoslyn said. "And thanks to the Matis Clan, protection from shaydes and ashenclaws will continue to be provided to the village we grew up in."

Zickar nodded. "We're happy to help in any way we can."

We passed a painting of Jaus standing on top of a dresalod carcass, a snarl on his face, and Rhoslyn jumped up to stroke the orc's cheek.

Jaus laughed and kissed her, and we continued walking.

We rounded another bend in the road and there it was, the big open market area with the bonfire blazing in the center, built to celebrate life.

"The fire is huge." I gaped at the towering mound of logs taking up a big part of the square.

As the flames flickered and cast a warm glow over the city, my heart thrummed along with the beat of drums. I started swaying my hips, eager to dance.

"The Flame Dance Festival has commenced," Jaus

announced in a loud voice, and orcs and humans alike cheered.

We surged forward to join everyone, only stopping when Nia cried out.

"Don't forget our surprise!"

She and Dakur lifted their pendants and blew across them at the same time, the low tone thrumming through the air, harmonizing with the beat of the drums.

Tiny lights erupted in the trees encircling the square in red, orange, yellow, and blue.

We all sighed at the beauty.

"Not bad, huh?" Nia asked, grinning up at Dakur. "We discovered that tone not long ago and frankly, I can't stop coaxing the leaves to shine for us."

"Blind us you mean," Dakur said with a laugh. "Sometimes, it's so bright after Nia's through that it's hard to sleep. But the lights fade in an hour or so."

"We can enjoy them until then," she said, holding out her hand. He took it and they rushed to join the crowd of dancers. Everyone else did too.

"Shall we dance, my amazing, heart-stopping, magnificent mate?" Turren asked, holding out his hand.

"We shall, my love." I nudged his hand aside and jumped into his arms, wrapping my legs around him while giving him a big kiss.

Then he carried me over to dance with our friends.

I hope you've enjoyed the Monster Mate Hunt Series!
I'm going to miss these people and this world.
What's next, you ask?
How about alien heroes who meet the women they'll
love forever?
Jump into the Brides of the Zuldrux Warriors Series
along with me with Book 1, Craved by the Alien Beast.
I've included chapter 1 here . . .

CRAVED BY THE ALIEN BEAST

I was stolen from Earth and gifted to an alien warrior. Will I find a new home with Aizor?

Vanessa: One minute, I'm working as a cook, the next, I've been abducted by robocops and sent to a distant planet where I'm attacked by a ferocious beast. Then a seven-foot-tall, blue-skinned alien rescues me with crystal spears slashing. He cuddles me in his arms, and I feel safe for the first time since fleeing my stalker ex.

Until he tosses me over his shoulder and takes me back to his clan where he announces I'm his new bride.

I'm determined to return home, but there's something about Aizor I can't resist. Am I falling for this muscle-bound alien with a killer smile?

Aizor: The crystal gods gifted me with Vanessa, and she's the prettiest being I've ever seen.

She's tiny.

Surprisingly snarly.

And she insists on returning to her home planet.

I have seven days to convince her to stay. I'll worship her. Massage her feet. And at night, I'll show her the gifts bestowed upon a Zuldrux warrior.

Then she'll accept she's my fated bride.

Craved by the Alien Beast is Book 1 of the Brides of the Zuldrux Warriors Series. Expect humor, size difference, devoted alien warriors who'll die to protect their fated mate, steamy romance, and a new alien world you'll want to live in.

Consent and HEA guaranteed.

Look for the rest of the Zuldrux Series!
Craved by the Alien Beast
Treasured by the Alien Rogue
Claimed by the Alien Barbarian
Cherished by the Alien Outlaw
Adored by the Alien Warlord

ABOUT THE AUTHOR

Ava Ross is a two-time *USA Today* Bestselling author who has written numerous titles, all of them featuring sweet and steamy romance. She fell for men with unusual features when she first watched Star Wars, where alien creatures have gone mainstream. She lives in New England with her husband (who is sadly not an alien, though he is still cute in his own way), her kids, and a few assorted pets.

Also by Ava Ross

Mail-Order Brides of Crakair

Brides of Driegon

Fated Mates of the Ferlaern Warriors

Fated Mates of the Xilan Warriors

Holiday with a Cu'zod Warrior

Galaxy Games

Alien Warrior Abandoned

Beastly Alien Boss

Bride of the Fae

A Sci-Fi Holiday Tail

Monsterville, USA

Monster on Board

(co-written with Alana Khan)

Love at First Orc

Monster Mate Hunt

Sweet Monster Treats

Brides of the Zuldrux Warriors

Monsters, PI

Single Titles

A Monster Worth Fighting For

Craving Stardust

Dad Bod Dragon

Mated to the Dragon

Jasmine's Grumpy Genie

Swamp Thing (You Make My Heart Sing)

You can find her books on Amazon.

CHAPTER 1
VANESSA

My boss, Franklin, rushed into the kitchen of Dria's Diner where I worked.

"You've gotta come see this on TV," he said. "It's happening!"

After sliding the burger I'd just finished cooking from the grill and onto a bun, adding the requested toppings and a generous side of fries, I slid the plate onto the window between the kitchen and the guest area of the diner.

I tapped the bell. "Order's up."

A server hustled over to grab the plate while I followed Franklin into the dining area and looked up at the TV mounted in the corner. Guests had stopped eating and gazed as raptly as Franklin at the screen.

"It's about the upcoming launch," he said. "You don't want to miss *this*."

"They're sending a bunch of scientists to Mars in a

few weeks," one of the customers seated on a high-top at the bar said, his face glowing in the yellow lights humming above the island. He braced his forearms on the shiny counter. "What of it? I can't see why tonight's special."

"They're testing the propulsion systems," Franklin said. "If they work, the project's a go. They've been loading supplies in the hull for months. The crew will ride partway in stasis, then the rest of the time, they'll check out the view of the stars. Marvel at planets they pass. Get ready to start building the new colony on Mars. It's basically Star Trek come to life. How can you not be as into that as me?"

"Beam me up?" a woman quipped from beside the guy at the island, and they clinked their drinks together, laughing.

Franklin's shoulders deflated, but only for a moment before he shored them up again with his never-ending excitement. "You know what I mean. After the systems are ready, it's just a matter of fine-tuning everything else and loading the nonperishable food inside. It's gonna be *real*. We're going to settle some people on Mars and form our first colony. I tell ya, if I was younger," he stroked back his thinning gray hair, "and fitter. And smarter. Well, I'd be volunteering to be one of the first settlers."

"They're only going to send people with the right skills," the woman said. "I doubt running a diner is one of them."

"In the olden days, people like me ran inns for travelers." Franklin's chest puffed with pride. "Pubs like my diner were valued. Mark my words, there'll be inns in the new settlement eventually. Stores and movie theaters. Dance halls." He frowned. "Maybe dance halls. People love that kind of thing, and they want the colony to feel like home."

As much as it could feel that way on a planet far from Earth. I wasn't sure if I'd go even if I was offered a spot, which I wouldn't be. I liked having my feet planted firmly on the ground. Besides, I'd never meet the stringent criteria. I wasn't a rocket scientist, and I was curvy. Okay, I was extra curvy.

"I think the whole thing is cool," I said. Franklin was a good guy, and there was no harm in supporting his latest hobby. "Can you imagine what it will look like? A red planet. Craters. New dishes to create from the vegetation they'll grow within the hydroponic chambers." I rubbed my hands together at the thought.

I was taking classes at the community college, studying culinary arts. I wanted to be a chef. There was nothing wrong with working at the diner. I was grateful for the job. But I kept dreaming about opening my own restaurant, of crafting amazing dishes in a pristine kitchen for people who'd rave about the spices I used and the perfect way I'd prepared a dish.

It wouldn't be in outer space, but I was more than okay with that.

"There's great wealth on Mars," Franklin gushed, warming to the subject. A few customers smiled, humoring him, but many nodded quite seriously. "All those new minerals. There must be gemstones and maybe even that planet's version of gold."

"I'm thinking of the plants and ways to test them to see if we can eat them," I said. "Someone could open up a restaurant there and serve all-Mars dishes."

Franklin nodded. "We could do it together."

Laughing, we high-fived each other.

After moving to Chicago, I could've done worse than land this job. Franklin had given me a chance and hadn't pressed hard when I told him I couldn't provide more than my driver's license for ID. On the run from a jerky ex, I'd left without much more than my coat and the wad of cash I'd stolen from his wallet. I'd hopped on a bus and planned to hide for the rest of my life—or until my ex forgot I'd ever existed.

On the TV, the camera crew panned back from the ship perched on the launching platform, gliding across the AI robocops guarding the high, electrified fence. The odds of anyone getting past the cops were pretty much zero, and even if you somehow did, the fence would fry you to a crisp.

AI robocops had been introduced by a billionaire entrepreneur about a year ago, and they'd quickly taken over most of our city's police protection units. They might cost a boatload of money to buy, but they didn't need much maintenance, they could work 24/7, and they explicitly followed the law. No more cops going rogue and killing some kid with a toy pistol or complaining because they didn't want to work overtime.

Now they patrolled the streets of all the major cities, and crime had gone way down. Who'd challenge a robot who could outrun, outthink, and outsmart you before you could finish committing the crime? We all felt a bunch safer.

The show ended on the TV, cutting to a commercial.

Franklin was lifting the remote to turn it down, and I was heading back to the kitchen to prepare new orders when the front door of the diner slammed open.

Robocops poured in, their electronic, glowing red eyes sweeping across the room.

A red bead of light lit up on my chest, and my hand froze on the door to the kitchen. I turned and backed against it, nearly falling into the room beyond.

The robocops whirred across the room, and as I scurried over to the wall beside the swinging door, two leaped over the counter. I gasped and lifted my hands, figuring they'd pass me and enter the kitchen. Like, maybe they wanted burgers. It was an inane thought, but it was all my frightened mind could come up with.

"Wait. What?" I yelped as the cops grabbed my arms, holding them tight enough to leave bruises. "I didn't do anything . . ."

Fuck, my ex had found me. I'd taken a chance using my driver's license to get this job and sign up for classes, thinking there was no way he could track me down, but it looked like he had.

Blubbering with fear and with my heart roaring up into my throat, I shrieked. My knees gave way.

I couldn't go back to him, couldn't let him throw me in jail.

One of the robocops poked my arm with something sharp, and the world swirled away . . .

Get Craved by the Alien Beast Now!